מיסודה

ArtScroll Youth Series®

Rabbi Nosson Scherman / Rabbi Meir Zlotowitz

General Editors

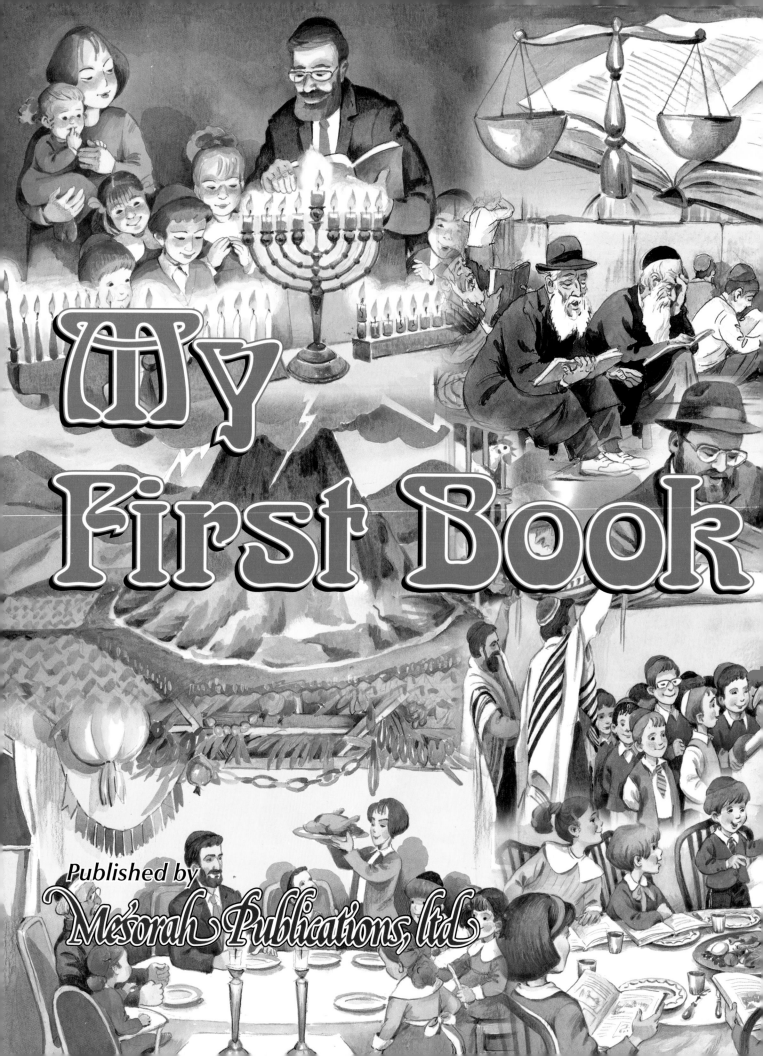

My First Book

Published by

Mesorah Publications, ltd.

# of Jewish Holidays

by Shmuel Blitz

Illustrated by Tova Katz

Introduction by Rabbi Nosson Scherman

*This book is dedicated to my sister, Phyllis
and her husband, Abe Frankel*

RTSCROLL YOUTH SERIES®

"MY FIRST BOOK OF JEWISH HOLIDAYS"

© *Copyright 2004 by* Mesorah Publications, Ltd.
First edition — First impression: March, 2004
    Second impression: February, 2012

Published by **MESORAH PUBLICATIONS, LTD.**
4401 Second Avenue / Brooklyn, N.Y 11232 / (718) 921-9000 / Fax: (718) 680-1875
www.artscroll.com

Distributed in Israel by SIFRIATI / A. GITLER
6 Hayarkon Street / Bnei Brak 51127

Distributed in Europe by LEHMANNS
Unit E, Viking Industrial Park, Rolling Mill Road / Jarrow, Tyne and Wear / England NE32 3DP

Distributed in Australia and New Zealand by GOLDS WORLD OF JUDAICA
3-13 William Street / Balaclava, Melbourne 3183, Victoria, Australia

Distributed in South Africa by KOLLEL BOOKSHOP
Shop 8A Norwood Hypermarket / Norwood 2196 / Johannesburg, South Africa

Printed in the United States of America by Noble Book Press Corp.
Custom bound by Sefercraft, Inc. / 4401 Second Avenue / Brooklyn N.Y. 11232

ISBN: 1-57819-998-0

Table of Contents

Times of Closeness
An Introduction by Rabbi Nosson Scherman

he first mitzvah given to the Jewish people as a nation was when Hashem commanded Moshe in Egypt to proclaim Rosh Chodesh, the new month. And when the Syrian-Greek king Antiochus tried to destroy the Jewish religion, one of the three mitzvos that he attacked was Rosh Chodesh. What is so special about Rosh Chodesh?

Rosh Chodesh does two things for the Jewish people: It makes it possible for us to have a calendar. And it reminds us that just as the moon seems to disappear and then renews itself each month, so too, the Jewish people always come back. Therefore, no matter how bad things may seem, we should not lose hope.

Let us look at these two lessons of Rosh Chodesh and see how important they are to us all the time.

Every year we look forward to Pesach, Rosh Hashanah and all the other festivals. The Torah calls them *moadim*, which means times when Jews have "meetings" with Hashem. They are also called *mikra'ei kodesh*, which means that the festivals are times when Hashem "invites" us to come closer to Him and to rejoice because of all the good things He has done for our ancestors and for us.

When Pesach comes, it is not just a history lesson about our freedom from Egypt. It is a time when we can still feel the same thrill that our ancestors felt when Moshe came and told them that they would no longer be slaves to Pharaoh and instead would go to Mount Sinai to receive the Torah and always be servants of Hashem. It is as if Hashem is telling us, "You can be free from all the troubles that the Jewish people have in the 21st century, just as the Jews were freed from their suffering in Egypt." On Shavuos, Hashem is telling us, "Come, My children. I gave you the Torah at Mount Sinai, and you can open your Chumash or Gemara today and see that the Torah is still yours, you can receive it again today."

Every Yom Tov is such a time. It tells us that we are still living in Jewish history.

But when do these Yamim Tovim take place? That is based on dates — dates on the calendar! If there were no Jewish calendar, there would be no festivals. That is why Rosh Chodesh is so important, and why it is the first mitzvah that Hashem gave us as a nation.

The Jewish calendar is based on the moon — because Hashem wants us to know that the Jewish people, like the moon, never get "old and worn out." Whenever it looked as if our history would be all over, we came back — just as there is a new moon every month. Even in the lifetime of our parents and grandparents, when nearly all of the yeshivos and Jewish communities of Europe were destroyed — it was like the moon disappearing at the end of the month — we came back. *Baruch Hashem*, there are strong and growing Jewish communities and yeshivos all over the world.

This book brings us the Jewish holidays, the stories behind them, and their laws and customs. It is filled with stories from the Torah, the Talmud, the Midrash, and our long and beautiful history. When we read this book, we feel that we are joining our forefathers as they left Egypt, standing with them at Mount Sinai, seeing Hashem's Clouds in the Desert and enjoying the thousand tastes of the *mann*. We join Mordechai and Esther in defeating Haman, and we are part of the Chashmonaim in defending the Torah against the Syrian-Greeks in the time of Chanukah. The laws and customs in this book show us that we must not only know what happened in the past, but how we should celebrate those miracles today.

We are grateful to Shmuel Blitz for creating this book. There is so much in it! And he does it so well! Tova Katz's illustrations make history live for us. All in all, this is a book that makes us proud to be part of Hashem's special people, a book to read and enjoy all year round.

Rosh Hashanah
CREATION

efore there were people, before there were animals, before there was the earth, before there were the skies and the oceans, even before there was light and darkness, there was nothing.

Then Hashem began creating.

On the first day Hashem created the Heavens and the Earth.

On the second day Hashem separated the skies and the waters above from the waters below.

Did You Know??
Hashem created the Torah before He created the world. The same way that an architect uses plans when he designs a building, Hashem used the Torah as His plan for creating the world.

On the third day Hashem created the grass, the plants, the crops, and the trees.

Also on the third day, Hashem created Gan Eden (where Adam and Chavah, the first people, would live on the first day of their lives).

Did You Know??
On the second day the angels were created. Also, Hashem created Gehinnom (punishment after death). That is one reason that when the second day was finished, the Torah does not say, "And it was good." Hashem was not pleased that there would be wicked people who have to be punished. Another reason is that even though Hashem made the Heavens on the second day, they were not completed until the third day.

Did You Know??
Hashem had still not created rain, so nothing was able to grow. It did not rain until man was created on the sixth day. This is because Hashem wanted man to pray for rain.

On the fourth day Hashem created the sun, the moon and the stars.

Did You Know??
At first, the sun and the moon were the same size, both shining equally bright. The moon was jealous and complained to Hashem, "How can the sun and I be the same size?" Hashem punished the moon for its complaint and made it smaller and less bright than the sun. But to make the moon feel better, Hashem created the stars, adding light at night.

On the fifth day Hashem created the fish and the birds.

A Closer Look
Hashem gave an extra blessing to birds and fish so that there would be huge amounts of them for man to eat. But animals did not receive this extra blessing when they were created, on the sixth day. Hashem did not want the snake to have this extra blessing because He knew that the snake would later bring trouble and pain to the world by persuading Chavah to sin.

Did You Know??
On the fifth day Hashem also created the Livyasan, the huge fish that lives in the ocean. Our Sages teach us that when Mashiach comes, Hashem will prepare a giant meal, that will be made from the *Livyasan*, for the *tzaddikim*.

On the sixth day Hashem created animals and Man.

A Closer Look

Why was Man created last? Hashem wanted everything in the world to be finished and ready before man was created, since it was all created for man. On the other hand, if a person could become too arrogant and proud, he can be told, "Everything, even the tiniest insect, was created before you were."

Every human being is descended from Adam and Chavah. No one can ever say, "I am better than you, because my ancestors were greater than yours!"

Before creating Man, Hashem said to the angels. "Let us make man." Some angels did not want Man created, while others did. But for Hashem, Man was the whole purpose of Creation.

Did You Know??

Some of our Sages say that Hashem took earth from the place where the *Beis HaMikdash* would one day be built, and used it to create Adam.

The sixth day of Creation was the first day of the month of Tishrei (Rosh Hashanah).

Ten things were created on that Friday, right before Shabbos. Some of these were: the rainbow that Noach would see after the Flood; the *mann* that the Jews ate in the desert after leaving Egypt; the rod that Moshe would use to do many miracles; the *shamir* insect that could eat through stone (King Shlomo used the *shamir* to cut the stones for the *Beis HaMikdash*); and the letters of the *Alef Beis*.

At the end of the sixth day Hashem finished creating, and on the seventh day He rested. This day is Shabbos, our most holy day.

Did You Know??

Shabbos is a special day, blessed by Hashem. Our Sages teach us that whoever honors the Shabbos is rewarded with a good life and riches.

Man receives an extra soul on Shabbos; the *"neshamah yeseirah."* This helps us make the Shabbos more joyous and holy. When Shabbos is over, this special *neshamah* leaves us, but it returns the following Shabbos.

A Closer Look

After Creation was finished, Shabbos came before Hashem. "Every day has a partner except me," Shabbos said. "Sunday has Monday, Tuesday has Wednesday and Thursday has Friday." "Do not worry," answered Hashem. "The Children of Israel will be your partner." If the Jewish People will watch over and guard the Shabbos, then Shabbos will protect the Jewish People.

Hashem placed Adam in the Garden of Eden. He saw that Adam was alone and created a wife for him. Adam named her Chavah, which means life. Adam said that she would be the mother of all human life.

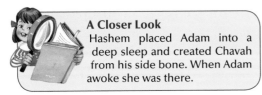

A Closer Look
Hashem placed Adam into a deep sleep and created Chavah from his side bone. When Adam awoke she was there.

A Closer Look
Whoever would eat the fruit from the Tree of Knowledge would acquire great wisdom and the understanding of good and evil. Whoever would eat from the Tree of Life would live forever.

The Garden of Eden was full of beautiful trees. There were two special trees there, the Tree of Knowledge and the Tree of Life.

Hashem told Adam and Chavah that they could eat from any tree in the entire Garden except for the Tree of Knowledge.

At that time, the snake had two regular legs, just like a person. It walked over to Chavah and asked, "Didn't Hashem tell you not to eat fruit from any trees of the Garden?" "No," replied Chavah, "Hashem said we *may* eat the fruits of the trees. But we may not even touch the Tree of Knowledge." "Touch it," said the snake. "You will see. Nothing will happen." The snake pushed Chavah against the Tree and she touched it. Sure enough, nothing happened.

"Just as nothing happened when you touched the tree," argued the snake, "nothing will happen when you eat the fruit of the Tree." And Chavah took the fruit of the Tree of Knowledge and ate it.

A Closer Look
Hashem never told Adam and Chavah not to touch the Tree. They were only not allowed to eat its fruit. Chavah ended up sinning because she added something in Hashem's Name that He did not say.

Chavah gave the fruit to Adam and he ate it, too.

Hashem punished Adam, Chavah and the snake. The snake became a cursed animal that would always crawl on the ground on its belly and it would not be able to taste food. It would be man's enemy, always trying to bite people, and people would try to kill snakes. Because of Chavah's sin, women would have pain when they had children. And because of Adam's sin, people would die. Man would also have to work hard to earn a living. Hashem sent Adam and Chavah out of the Garden of Eden.

Hashem judged Adam and Chavah on Rosh Hashanah. We, too, are judged on Rosh Hashanah. On Rosh Hashanah it is decided who shall live and who shall die; who shall be sick and who shall be cured; who would be rich and who would be poor; which countries would have peace and which ones would go to war.

Did You Know??
Adam and Eve sinned and were sent out of the Garden of Eden on the very same day they were created, Friday afternoon before Shabbos. Some say they were allowed to stay for Shabbos and were sent away right after Shabbos.

Two children were born to Chavah — Kayin and Hevel. Kayin was a farmer and Hevel was a shepherd. They both brought offerings to thank Hashem for His blessings. Kayin was the first one to bring an offering, but he did not bring his best fruit. Hevel brought his nicest animals. Hashem accepted Hevel's offering but not Kayin's. Kayin became jealous and killed Hevel.

Adam lived for 930 years.

A Closer Look

After Kayin killed Hevel, Hashem said, "You are a wicked person, Kayin. Not only did you destroy your brother, but you destroyed all the future generations that would have been born to him." Hashem punished Kayin. He sent him wandering throughout the world. Kayin would never again have a steady home, and it would be hard for him to grow food from the ground. Kayin begged Hashem for mercy, and Hashem pitied him. He placed a mark upon his head so that people would know not to harm him.

Did You Know??

Adam was supposed to live 1000 years. But before Adam was created, Hashem showed him all his future descendants. He saw King David, who was supposed to live for only three hours. "How can such a holy soul live for only three hours?" Adam asked. "Please, Hashem, give him seventy years of my life." Hashem agreed. Adam died at the age of 930 and David HaMelech lived 70 years.

A Closer Look

On Rosh Hashanah, when Hashem finished creating the Universe, He became its King.

LAWS OF ROSH HASHANAH

1. During Elul, the month before Rosh Hashanah, we begin preparations for Rosh Hashanah by doing *teshuvah* (repentance).

A Closer Look
Hashem accepts our prayers and our *teshuvah* all year. But the month of Elul is an especially good time for Hashem to hear our prayers.

Did You Know??
Sephardic Jews say *Selichos* (prayers of repentence) every day of Elul (except Shabbos). Ashkenazic Jews begin saying *Selichos* several days before Rosh Hashanah.

2. During the month of Elul Ashkenazi communities blow the shofar every morning after *Shacharis* (except on Shabbos and Erev Rosh Hashanah). Some also blow it after *Minchah*.

A Closer Look
The sound of the shofar calls to us to do *teshuvah* during Elul. It reminds us that on the first day of Elul, when Moshe went up to Har Sinai to receive the second set of *Luchos* (the Tablets with the Ten Commandments), they blew the shofar. They did this to announce that Moshe went up and that the Jews should not sin again as they did the first time he received the Ten Commandments, when they made the Golden Calf.

3. Rosh Hashanah is the day we are judged by Hashem. It is when He decides what kind of year we will have. Hashem decides who will live and who will die, who will be sick and who will be healthy, who will be poor and who will be rich.

A Closer Look
We can never know for sure how Hashem will judge us. But if we pray properly to Hashem and do *teshuvah*, we can feel confident that we will be inscribed in the Book of Life for a good and healthy year.

4. The Torah commands us to blow the shofar on Rosh Hashanah. It is proper to hear 100 blasts from the shofar. There are three types of sounds we make with the shofar, *tekiah, shevarim* and *teruah*. A *tekiah* is one long sound, a *shevarim* is three shorter sounds, and a *teruah* is nine short sounds.

A Closer Look

The shofar is the horn of a ram. It reminds us of the ram that *Avraham Avinu* sacrificed to Hashem instead of his son Yitzchak. We pray to Hashem that in the merit of Avraham and Yitzchak, we should be saved and be given a good year.

Also, our Sages teach us that we blow the shofar twice -- once before *Mussaf* and once again during *Mussaf*. This confuses the Satan. When he sees how hard we try to do Hashem's mitzvos, he will think that we deserve to hear the shofar of the Mashiach.

Did You Know??

If the first day of Rosh Hashanah comes out on Shabbos, we do not blow the shofar that day. This is so that no one will make a mistake and carry a shofar outside on Shabbos. The second day of Rosh Hashanah never comes out on Shabbos, so we always blow the shofar on that day.

5. Rosh Hashanah is considered a *Yom Tov*, a day of joy. When we leave shul we should feel sure that Hashem will grant us a healthy and happy year. We go home and eat and drink just as we would on any other *Yom Tov*, even though it is a serious day.

A Closer Look

Our Sages teach us that if we do *teshuvah* (repentance), give *tzedakah* (charity), and pray hard *(tefillah)*, we can actually get a bad decree changed.

6. It is customary to greet people on the first night of Rosh Hashanah by saying, *"L'shanah tovah tikaseivu v'seichaseimu."*

Did You Know??

This means "You should be written and sealed for a good year." We are wishing everyone a happy and healthy New Year.

7. It is customary not to sleep during the day of Rosh Hashanah. People learn Torah or recite *Tehillim* after the meal.

8. On the night of Rosh Hashanah we dip the first piece of challah that we eat into honey. After the challah has been eaten, we dip a piece of apple into honey, make a *berachah* on the apple, and eat it. We make a special request that Hashem give us a sweet new year.

A Closer Look
We do this to show that we hope Hashem will give us a year as sweet as honey.

Did You Know??
It is customary to use round challos on Rosh Hashanah.

9. It is a custom to eat certain foods on the night of Rosh Hashanah. Either the names or something else about these foods symbolizes something good for the coming year. Before we eat these foods we ask Hashem for the things that each food symbolizes. Some of these foods are • carrots, • cabbage, • beets, • dates, • pomegranates, • fish, • the head of a ram, lamb, or fish, • pumpkin.

Did You Know??
There are different reasons for eating these symbolic foods. Some of the foods are sweet tasting (so that we will have a sweet year), some of their names — in Hebrew, Aramaic or other languages — refer to abundance and plenty (so that we will have a year filled with mitzvos and success), or to destruction (so that our enemies will be destroyed).

10. On the first afternoon of Rosh Hashanah, after *Minchah,* we go to a body of water and say *Tashlich*.

Did You Know??
Tashlich is a prayer in which we symbolically throw our sins into the water.
If the first day of Rosh Hashanah comes out on Shabbos, we say Tashlich on the second day. If a river is too far, or if there is no time on Rosh Hashanah, Tashlich may be said on any day until Yom Kippur. Some even say it until Hoshanah Rabbah.

Yom Kippur

Hashem Forgives the Jewish People Completely

t was the seventh day in the month of Sivan. A holy cloud had been covering Mount Sinai since Rosh Chodesh. There was absolute silence. Not a bird chattered, not a dog barked, and not one leaf blew in the wind. Hashem began speaking the words of the Ten Commandments. "I am Hashem, your G-d," He said. He continued with the second Commandment. But the sound of Hashem's Voice was so holy and frightening that the people were scared to listen. They begged Moshe to recite the rest of the Ten Commandments himself, and he did.

Hashem then took Moshe up to heaven. He stayed there forty days and forty nights. During that time, Hashem taught him the whole Torah. The fortieth day was the sixteenth day of Tammuz. Many people expected Moshe to come down from the mountain on the sixteenth of Tammuz. But they made a mistake. He wasn't supposed to come until the *next* day. They thought Moshe was dead! They made a Golden Calf to take Moshe's place.

When Moshe came down and saw the people dancing around the Golden Calf, he smashed the Ten Commandments at the foot of the mountain. Then he took the Calf and ground it up into dust. "Whoever is for Hashem, come and join me," Moshe called out. The whole tribe of Levi came to Moshe. Three thousand people who worshiped the Golden Calf were killed that day.

Did You Know??
The seventeenth day of Tammuz was the day Moshe smashed the Ten Commandments. It became a sad day for the Jewish People for all time. Among other tragedies that happened on the 17th of Tammuz, the Romans broke through the outer wall of Jerusalem before destroying the Second *Beis HaMikdash*.

A Closer Look
How could it be that so soon after seeing all the miracles that Hashem did for them in Egypt and in the desert, the people began worshiping an idol? It was because Moshe did not come when they thought he would. They were afraid that they had no leader and they wanted something that would connect them with Hashem. This made Hashem very angry, since it was forbidden to create or worship such an image.

On the 19th of Tammuz Moshe climbed back up Mount Sinai to beg Hashem to forgive the Jewish People's terrible sin of the Golden Calf. He remained on the mountain another forty days and forty nights, begging Hashem to forgive His people.

Then, on the 29th day of Av, Moshe came down the mountain a second time. He had obtained Hashem's forgiveness for the Jewish People. "Carve a new pair of stone Tablets," Hashem commanded Moshe, "and I will write the Ten Commandments on them." Moshe climbed back up the mountain. Hashem taught him the Torah again.

After being on Mount Sinai a third time for another forty days, Moshe came down from the mountain with the new Tablets of the Ten Commandments. He told the people, "Hashem has now forgiven you."

The day Moshe came down the mountain with the new Tablets was the tenth day of Tishrei. That day would become Yom Kippur. It would be a day of forgiveness for the Jewish People for all time.

Moshe now gave the people the second Tablets of the Ten Commandments. His face shone with a holy light, and the people were afraid to approach him. Because of that, Moshe covered his face whenever he taught Torah to the Jewish People, but he uncovered his face when he spoke to Hashem.

Moshe now began to teach the people the entire Torah — the Laws of Hashem.

A Closer Look
The first 40 days that Moshe was with Hashem on Mount Sinai was a good time. Hashem was happy with His people. The second forty days was a bad time; Hashem was angry with His people because of the sin of the Golden Calf. The third forty-day period was again a good time. Hashem forgave His people and was once again happy with them.

Did You Know??
The Torah tells us that Hashem spoke to Moshe "face to face" — directly. Moshe had a closer relationship with Hashem than any other person.

Today, people stay in shul the entire day of Yom Kippur, and pray to Hashem that they be sealed in the Book of Life. We pray for a year of happiness, success, and health.

A Closer Look
Rav Yisroel Salanter taught that if we were only given Yom Kippur once every seventy years as a time to be forgiven by Hashem, it would be a wonderful gift. How grateful we should be that Hashem gives us Yom Kippur every single year as a time to do *teshuvah* and be forgiven for our sins!

Did You Know??
In the time of the *Beis HaMikdash*, a special Yom Kippur service was performed. It was the one day a year the Kohen Gadol would enter the Holy of Holies. Today, Yom Kippur is still a special day of fasting, prayer, and forgiveness.

LAWS OF YOM KIPPUR

1. The first ten days of the Jewish year, starting with the first day of Rosh Hashanah and ending on Yom Kippur, are called *Aseres Y'mei Teshuvah* — The Ten Days of Repentance.

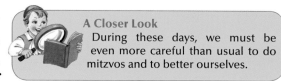

A Closer Look
During these days, we must be even more careful than usual to do mitzvos and to better ourselves.

2. In most communities, sometime between Rosh Hashanah and Yom Kippur, people perform *kaparos*. Either a chicken or money is waved above the head, and a prayer is said.

Did You Know??
This reminds us that we deserve to be punished for our sins, and symbolizes that the chicken or money should take the place of our being punished. If a chicken is used, the bird or its cost is given to poor people. If money is used, it is given to charity.

3. Before Yom Kippur we should ask people to forgive us just in case we did something bad to them — on purpose, or even by accident.

A Closer Look
On Yom Kippur we do *teshuvah* and ask Hashem to forgive us for our sins. But how can we ask Him to forgive us, if we have sinned against other people? We first must get forgiveness from the people we hurt.
On the other hand, how can we ask Hashem to forgive us if we have not forgiven others who have asked us for forgiveness? If we forgive others, we hope that Hashem will surely forgive us as well.

4. There is a special mitzvah to eat on
   Erev Yom Kippur.

5. During *Minchah* of Erev Yom Kippur,
   we say the same *Viduy* (confession)
   that we will say on Yom Kippur itself.

A Closer Look
The Sages want us to say this *Viduy* before Yom Kippur in case it becomes impossible for us to say it on Yom Kippur.

6. Before going to shul on
   Erev Yom Kippur, par-
   ents bless their children.

A Closer Look
The holiness of Yom Kippur has already begun, and the Gates of Mercy and Repentance are already open. Parents pray that their children will be granted a good and healthy life.

7. Men wear a *kittel* throughout the prayers, on both the night and day of Yom Kippur.

Did You Know??
The white *kittel* gives us an angel-like appearance. The *kittel* also reminds us of the white shrouds a person wears when he is buried. On Yom Kippur we realize that everyone will die one day, and we will then have to stand before Hashem and be judged for everything we did, both good and bad.
  Some people wear a *kittel* on Rosh Hashanah as well.

8. On Yom Kippur it is forbidden to eat, drink, wash ourselves, or wear leather shoes. Any work that is forbidden on Shabbos is also forbidden on Yom Kippur.

Did You Know??
In the times of the *Beis HaMikdash*, there was a special service for the Kohen Gadol to perform in the *Beis HaMikdash* on Yom Kippur. At the completion of this service, Hashem would let the nation know if they were forgiven. If they were, there was great happiness, dancing, and rejoicing throughout the land.

9. It is permitted to wear "shoes" made of either rubber, cloth, or other non-leather materials on Yom Kippur.

Did You Know??
Some types of sneakers contain leather and may not be worn on Yom Kippur.

10. During the Ten Days of Repentance, and on Yom Kippur itself, we greet each other by saying "*G'mar chasimah tovah.*"

Did You Know??
These words mean, "May you be sealed for good." We hope the other person is sealed in the Book of Life and that only good things will happen to him.

11. On Yom Kippur we try to put as much effort as we can into our *davening*.

12. If someone is sick, a rabbi should be asked whether or not that person should fast. Under no circumstances is a person allowed to put his life in danger by fasting.

Did You Know??
One year, a plague of cholera (a very dangerous, life-threatening disease) spread throughout the city of Vilna. Rav Yisrael Salanter announced that everyone must eat on Yom Kippur so they do not become weak and catch the deadly disease. He himself walked up to the *bimah*, made *Kiddush* and ate.

13. Before Yom Kippur ends, we say an additional prayer service — *Ne'ilah*.

A Closer Look
Ne'ilah means "closing." This is our last chance to pray before the Heavenly Gates of Repentance that were open wide through the month of Elul and the *Aseres Yemei Teshuvah* are closed.

Did You Know??
At the end of Ne'ilah the shofar is sounded. Some blow one long blast, others have different customs.

14. Every month we say *Kiddush Levanah*, a special blessing to Hashem about the Moon. There is a custom to say *Kiddush Levanah* right after Yom Kippur.

A Closer Look
Some people prefer to bless the moon during *Aseres Y'mei Teshuvah*, so that they will have another mitzvah to their credit before Yom Kippur arrives.

Succos

Hashem Protects the Jewish People in the Desert

fter being freed from Egypt, the Jewish People began their journey in the desert toward *Eretz Yisrael*. This was the land that Hashem had promised them; a land flowing with milk and honey. He took them out of Egypt, split the Sea of Reeds (See Pesach, page 56) and then brought them to Mount Sinai where they received the Torah (see Shavuos, page 74).

"I am sending an angel in front of you to guide and protect you on your way to *Eretz Yisrael*," Hashem told the people. "If you listen to My laws, you will arrive there quickly and safely."

As soon as the journey in the desert began, Hashem protected the people with the *Ananei Hakavod* — Clouds of Glory. They protected the people from all harm and discomfort in the desert — from the sun during the day, and from the cold at night. The people built themselves *succos*, or booths, as well.

A Closer Look

The Torah tells us, "Your children shall dwell in *succos* (booths) for seven days, so that they will know that I had you live in booths when I took you out of Egypt." Our sages teach that when we sit in the succah we should think about how Hashem protected us with those Clouds of Glory. We should also think of the actual booths that the Jewish People built in the desert.

Hashem commanded the people to build a *Mishkan* and He told Moshe how it should be built. After the first Yom Kippur in the desert, it would be Hashem's "dwelling place" on earth while they traveled in the desert. The people would offer sacrifices there, and the Kohanim would perform the holy service. All the people brought contributions that were used to build the *Mishkan*.

Did You Know??
They started building the Mishkan the day after Yom Kippur and finished making all the parts on the twenty-fifth of Kislev. But Hashem did not tell Moshe to put up the *Mishkan* for regular use until Rosh Chodesh Nissan. The twenty-fifth of Kislev would later become the first day of Chanukah.

Finally, when the Mishkan was ready, the people began their journey away from Mount Sinai. They traveled for three days with the Holy Ark in front of them, and the Clouds of Glory protecting them.

Did You Know??
The Torah mentions the Clouds of Glory seven times. This teaches us that seven separate clouds protected the Jewish People. There was one cloud on each of the people's four sides, a fifth cloud above to protect them from the sun, a sixth cloud below to protect their feet, and a seventh cloud in front which flattened the ground and killed the dangerous snakes and scorpions, which are common in the desert.

While traveling with the Ark, Moshe would say, "Rise up, Hashem, and let Your enemies be divided and destroyed. Let those who hate You run away from You." When the people stopped traveling, and the Ark was set down, Moshe would say, "Dwell, Hashem, among the many thousands of Your people, Israel."

Each day the *mann* would appear on the ground for the people to eat.

A Closer Look
The *mann* was shaped like a seed, and had a white color. It had the taste of whatever the person wanted it to taste like. No matter how much a person tried to gather, every person got the same amount, and if it was saved overnight it would spoil. On Friday, though, every person received a a double-portion of *mann* — one for Friday and one for Shabbos, when people are not allowed to carry outside.

The Jews should have gone directly to *Eretz Yisrael* after building the *Mishkan.* Moshe sent twelve spies to scout out the land of Israel. The spies were very important men, the leaders of the tribes.

"Go see if the people in the land of Israel are weak or strong," Moshe told them. "See if the land is good for planting."

After forty days the spies returned. "We arrived in the land and it is indeed a land that flows with milk and honey. But the people who live there are strong and they live in great, fortified cities. We even saw giants! We look like grasshoppers compared to them! We will not be able to defeat them!"

Two of the spies, Yehoshua and Calev, stood up and said, "The land we saw is very, very good. And if Hashem wants us to conquer it, then we will. Do not rebel against Hashem and do not be afraid of these people!" But the people did not believe them. They became very frightened and cried that whole night. "Let us find a new leader to take us back to Egypt where we will be safe."

It was a great sin for the people not to trust Hashem. "The spies who said bad things about the Land will die in a plague," Hashem decreed. "The nation will wander in the desert for forty years, and all of those who did not trust in Me will die. Only their children will be able to enter the Land. Yehoshua and Calev will also enter *Eretz Yisrael* and receive their inheritance."

A Closer Look
The night that the people cried was the ninth day of Av. Because the Jews cried on that night — Tishah B'Av — Hashem decreed that it would always remain a sad day for the Jews.

Hashem continued to protect the people in the desert. He gave them a well in the merit of Miriam, Moshe's sister. The people always had enough to drink. But toward the end of the forty years, Miriam died, and the well dried up. "Why have you brought us to this desert to die of thirst?" the people complained.

Hashem told Moshe, "Take your stick and speak to the rock. Then there will be water for the people."

"You rebel against Hashem!" Moshe said to the people. He lifted his stick and struck the rock. Water came gushing forth for the people to drink.

A Closer Look
The Jewish People had been wandering in the desert for close to forty years. As long as Miriam was alive, the well followed them. When she died, the well dried up. This teaches us how we are often saved and protected through the merit of righteous people.

Did You Know??
Hashem told Moshe to speak to the rock, but he hit the rock. Because he did not do what Hashem told him, Moshe was punished. He was not able to enter *Eretz Yisrael*. He died with the rest of his generation in the Wilderness. This shows how careful we must be to follow the commandments of Hashem exactly.

Once, Bilaam, the wicked prophet of the gentiles, came to curse the Jews. But Hashem again protected the Jews in the desert. He forced Bilaam to bless the people. Hashem would let no harm come to His people.

At the age of 120, Moshe died in the desert. Forty years after they left Egypt, the Jewish People, led by Moshe's student Yehoshua, entered the Land of Israel.

The holiday of Succos is called *Z'man Simchaseinu* — the time of our joy. After doing *teshuvah* during Elul, Rosh Hashanah and Yom Kippur, we celebrate our hope that we have been forgiven and have been granted a good new year.

Pesach, when we were freed from Egypt, is the first festival we celebrated. Then we celebrated Shavuos, when we received of the Torah. Succos completes the series of festivals.

The Torah also calls Succos *Chag Ha'asif,* the festival of gathering. Succos comes at the end of the summer, when we finish harvesting the crops, and food is gathered up and put away for the long, cold winter. This is another reason for joy.

LAWS OF SUCCOS

1. It is customary to start building a succah the night after Yom Kippur.

A Closer Look
We want to go from one mitzvah to another. Also, to show that our *teshuvah* on Yom Kippur was sincere, we make sure to start a new mitzvah right away.

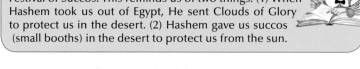

Did You Know??
The Torah commands us to live in the succah during the Festival of Succos. This reminds us of two things: (1) When Hashem took us out of Egypt, He sent Clouds of Glory to protect us in the desert. (2) Hashem gave us succos (small booths) in the desert to protect us from the sun.

2. The walls of the succah must be strong enough not to be blown around by a normal wind.
3. The roof of the succah is made of *s'chach*.

Did You Know??
Basically, *s'chach* can be made out of anything that grew from the ground, except for food. However, the *s'chach* cannot still be growing from the ground. Enough *s'chach* should be put on the roof so that there is more shade than light at midday, when the sun is very bright; but it is best if the *s'chach* is still loose enough so that you can see stars when you look up at night.

4. Most people hang beautiful decorations in the succah.

A Closer Look
We should always try to make every mitzvah as beautiful as possible.

5. The Torah teaches that we should live in the succah for seven days, just as we live in our houses. Unless the weather is very bad, we should eat in the succah, sleep there, and also study there.

A Closer Look
We are commanded to live in the succah during the month of Tishrei, even though Hashem began protecting us with His Clouds of Glory in the month of Nissan, when He took us out of Egypt.
The reason is that Nissan is in the spring, when many people move outside to spend time outdoors. Tishrei is in autumn, when it is getting colder. This shows everyone that we are moving into our succah because Hashem commanded us to, not because the weather is nice.

6. When we eat in the succah, we say the blessing,

בָּרוּךְ אַתָּה ה׳ אֱלֹהֵינוּ מֶלֶךְ הָעוֹלָם, אֲשֶׁר קִדְּשָׁנוּ בְּמִצְוֹתָיו וְצִוָּנוּ לֵישֵׁב בַּסֻּכָּה.

Blessed are You, Hashem, our God, King of the universe, Who has made us holy with His mitzvos, and has commanded us to live in the succah.''

A Closer Look
A great rabbi used to say: "I can enter the succah with every part of my body; even with the mud on my shoes." He meant to say that unlike other mitzvos, staying in the succah involved his whole body, not just a part of it. He also meant that Succos is a chance to get closer to Hashem, even though we may be stained with sins.

7. The Torah commands us to take a *lulav* (a frond from a date palm), an *esrog* (a citron), *haddasim* (myrtle branches), and *aravos* (willows) on Succos. The accepted custom is take three *haddasim* and two *aravos*.

Did You Know??
The *lulav, esrog, haddasim,* and *aravos* together are called the *"Arba'ah Minim"* — The Four Species.
The *esrog,* which has both a nice smell and taste, is like a *tzaddik*. A *tzaddik* studies Torah and does good deeds.
The branch of the *lulav* tree (a date palm), whose fruit tastes good but does not have a pleasant smell, is like someone who studies Torah but does not do good deeds.
The *haddasim,* which smell good but have no taste, are like someone who doesn't study Torah but does good deeds.
The *aravos,* which have no smell and no taste, are like someone who neither studies Torah nor does good deeds.
When we hold all four of them together we show that all Jews are always united as one.

8. Every day of Succos, except for Shabbos, we take the Four Species. The *lulav, haddasim* and *aravos* are tied together, with the *lulav* in the center. With the "spine" of the *lulav* facing us, the three *haddasim* should be to the right, and the two *aravos* to the left. We pick up this bundle in our right hand, and we pick up the *esrog,* upside-down, in our left. We make the *berachah* and turn the *esrog* right-side-up. We then wave the Four Species in all six directions (the four sides, up, and down). There are different customs about the order of these directions.

A Closer Look
Each of the *arba'ah Minim* is shaped like a different part of the body. The *esrog* is shaped like the heart, the *lulav* is shaped like the spine, the *haddasim* are shaped like the eyes, and the *aravos* are shaped like the mouth. When we wave the *arba'ah minim* together, we show that we want to serve Hashem with all our heart and our entire body.

Did You Know??
A left-handed person takes the lulav in his left hand and the esrog in his right hand.

9. *Ushpizin* means guests. It is a mitzvah to invite guests to our Yom Tov meals. But the succah is so holy that we can also invite seven special guests into our succah each day. These special guests are the seven leaders of our Nation: Avraham, Yitzchak, Yaakov, Yosef, Moshe, Aharon, and David *HaMelech*.

Did You Know??
We receive a very special reward for living in the succah on Succos: the privilege of inviting and welcoming the *Shechinah* (Hashem's holy Presence), and also these seven special guests, into our succah.

10. In shul, on the first six days of Succos (except for Shabbos), everyone takes his Four Species and marches around the *bimah* during the morning prayers, while saying a prayer called *Hoshanos*.

11. On the seventh day, called Hoshanah Rabbah, all the *Sifrei Torah* are taken out of the *Aron Kodesh* and held at the *bimah*. Everyone (except those holding a Torah) marches around the *bimah* seven times, while holding the *arba'ah minim* and saying the *Hoshanos* prayers. Then each person takes a bundle of five *aravah* branches and hits it on the ground.

Did You Know??
Some people have the custom to stay awake the entire night of Hoshanah Rabbah to study Torah. On this night, a final seal is put on our judgment from Yom Kippur.

A Closer Look
In the *Beis Hamikdash*, the people used to walk around the *Mizbei'ach*, the Altar, holding aravah branches.

12. The eighth day of Succos is another *Yom Tov*. It is called Shemini Atzeres.

A Closer Look
In Nusach sefard communities, all the *sifrei Torah* are taken out of the *Aron Kodesh* and carried around the bimah seven times (this is called *hakafos*) after *Maariv*. During each of these seven times, people sing and dance to show their great love for the Torah.

Did You Know??
In *Eretz Yisrael*, Hoshanah Rabbah is the last day we sit in the succah. Outside of Eretz Yisrael, most people eat their meals in the Succah on Shemini Atzeres, but do not recite the succah blessing. On Simchas Torah we no longer eat in the succah.

13. On Shemini Atzeres we say the prayer for rain, *Tefillas Geshem*.

A Closer Look
In *Eretz Yisrael* it almost never rains between Pesach and Succos. Therefore, it is very important that it rain during the winter months, so there will be enough water for the crops and for drinking. Jews throughout the world say this special prayer on Shemini Atzeres, asking Hashem to provide enough rain during the coming winter.

14. Simchas Torah means "the celebration of the Torah." This is the name given to the day we finish reading the last section of the Torah. We make a big celebration in shul, and also immediately start the Torah all over again from *Bereishis*. In Eretz Yisrael, Simchas Torah and Shemini Atzeres are the same day. Outside of Eretz Yisrael, Simchas Torah is the day after Shemini Atzeres.

Did You Know??
On Simchas Torah, there are *Hakafos* in the evening and again in the morning. In most communities, every man and boy is called up to the Torah. All the young children are called up to the Torah as a group. They stand under a big *tallis,* and say the *berachah* together with an adult. In many shuls, even children under the age of bar mitzvah get called up to the Torah individually.

Chanukah
Rededicating the *Beis HaMikdash*

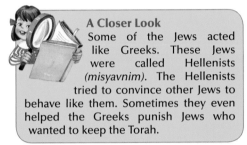ntiochus was a Syrian-Greek king who ruled the land of Israel about 200 years after the building of the Second *Beis HaMikdash*. He was very evil. He stole gold and silver vessels from the *Beis HaMikdash* and even entered the Holy of Holies. "I will not let the Jewish people worship Hashem," he decreed. "All Jews must act like Greeks, and worship our idols and gods." He had an idol put inside the *Beis HaMikdash*.

He made laws that Jewish babies could not have a *bris,* and that no one was allowed to keep Shabbos or Rosh Chodesh. No one was allowed to learn Torah. Many Jews chose death instead of worshiping the Greek idols.

A Closer Look
Some of the Jews acted like Greeks. These Jews were called Hellenists *(misyavnim)*. The Hellenists tried to convince other Jews to behave like them. Sometimes they even helped the Greeks punish Jews who wanted to keep the Torah.

Did You Know??
Among the brave people who refused to become Hellenists were Chanah and her seven sons. King Antiochus wanted them to bow down to an idol. Each son refused and was tortured and killed, one after the other. Chanah, the mother, encouraged her sons to follow the laws of Hashem. After all seven sons were killed she herself climbed up onto a roof, and jumped to her death. A heavenly voice was heard, "The mother of these children is happy."

Outside the city of Jerusalem, in the town of Modi'in, lived a man named Matisyahu. He was a Kohen. One day, soldiers of the king came to Modi'in. "Matisyahu," they barked, "King Antiochus demands that you follow the ways of the Hellenists and no longer follow the laws of your Torah. He wants you to sacrifice a pig on his altar. If you do it, the king will make you very rich." Matisyahu would never do such a thing.

Just then, a Jewish man approached the altar and began to sacrifice a pig to the Greek idol. Matisyahu became furious. He grabbed a sword and killed the Jewish man right there. Then he killed all the soldiers.

"Whoever is for Hashem come with me!" he called to the Jews.

Matisyahu and his five sons, together with many followers, left all their possessions and went off to the mountains. There, they were able to follow the laws of Hashem and also prepare for war against Antiochus.

Six thousand Jews joined Matisyahu's army. At night they would attack the Syrian-Greeks and destroy their idols and their army bases.

Matisyahu was an old man. Before he died, he called his five sons together and told them, "Continue to follow the ways of Hashem and do not give up this fight. All Jews must be able to follow the laws of the Torah without fear."

Matisyahu's son Judah led this group of brave soldiers. His followers were called Maccabees.

Did You Know??
There are a few possible reasons why the Jewish army were called Maccabees. One reason is that they were named after the word מַקֶּבֶת (makevet) which means hammer. Some suggest that the word מַכַּבִּי (Maccabee) stands for the words מִי כָּמוֹךָ בָּאֵלִים ה׳, which means "Who is like You among the strong ones, O Hashem!" Another explanation is that the word מַכַּבִּי might be an abbreviation for מַתִּתְיָהוּ כֹּהֵן בֶּן יוֹחָנָן, Matisyahu the Kohen, son of Yochanan.

Did You Know??
During the revolt of the Maccabim, there was a Jewish woman named Yehudis. She went to the tent of Holofernes, the Syrian-Greek general, where she fed him large amounts of cheese to make him thirsty. Then she gave him wine, which made him drunk and tired. When he fell asleep, she cut off his head. When the Greek soldiers saw their general was dead, they ran away in fear.

Once, a large army of Syrian-Greek soldiers were marching towards the Maccabees. The Jews were afraid and trembled. "We are a small and weak group of men. How can we fight this large army?" they asked.

Judah remembered his father's words. "If we trust in Hashem," he told the people, "there is no difference whether we are a large army or a small army. Hashem will help us defeat the enemy!"

Judah and the Maccabees won battle after battle against the great Syrian-Greek army. The Syrian-Greeks went back home in shame.

Judah said to the Jewish people, "Praised is Hashem. Let us now go up to the *Beis HaMikdash,* cleanse it of all the idols and once again make it holy to Him."

They climbed up to the Temple Mount. There, they saw weeds and grass growing from the floor and walls of the *Beis HaMikdash*. Everyone joined in and worked very hard, scrubbing and cleaning the entire area.

They built a new Altar of stones, but saw that the Menorah had been stolen. The Kohanim took seven iron rods, covered them with zinc, and built a new Menorah.

"But where will we find pure olive oil to light the Menorah?" they asked Judah. They searched everywhere, but all the oil they found was no longer pure. Finally, they found one jar of oil that still had the seal of the Kohen Gadol on it. It was pure! "We have enough oil to light for just one day," said the Kohanim. "It will take us eight days to prepare new oil." But a great miracle occurred. The small amount of pure oil burned for the entire eight days, until the Kohanim were able to prepare new oil. The people were filled with joy and danced and prayed to Hashem, thanking Him.

The Jews lit their new Menorah on the twenty-fifth day of Kislev. The next year, the Rabbis made an eight-day holiday in honor of this special miracle. This holiday is called Chanukah.

A Closer Look
Open up *Sefer Bereishis* in the Torah, and count each word until you reach the 25th word. That word is אור, which means *light*. This is a hint in the Torah to Chanukah, which is celebrated on the 25th of Kislev.

Did You Know??
The word Chanukah means "dedication." The holiday was called Chanukah because the Jewish People once again dedicated the *Beis HaMikdash* and were able to offer sacrifices. Also, the word Chanukah is a combination of the words *"Chanu"* which means "they rested," and the letters "chaf" and "heh", which equal twenty-five in Hebrew. The Jews were victorious and rested from the war on the twenty-fifth day of Kislev.

LAWS OF CHANUKAH

1. On Chanukah, which begins on the twenty-fifth day of the month of Kislev, we light a menorah every night for eight nights. The head of the household can light for the entire family. In most families, all the men and boys light their own menorahs. In many families, the girls light also. In Ashkenazic communities, it is customary for everyone in the family — except for a woman whose husband is lighting for her — to light his or her own menorah.

2. On the first night of Chanukah, we light the flame on the far right of the menorah plus the *shamash* (an extra candle, separate from the others). On each of the following nights, a new flame is added. The new flame is lit first. On the eighth night, all eight plus the *shamash* are lit.

Did You Know??
There are two places to put the menorah. It can be lit in a place where people outside the house can see it. In this way we show the world that a great miracle happened and everyone should know about it. Or the menorah may be lit inside, in a doorway opposite the *mezuzah*. Then we have mitzvos on both sides of us — the menorah on the left side and the *mezuzah* on the right.

3. Either candles or oil may be used for lighting the menorah, but it is better to use olive oil.

4. The Chanukah lights are not allowed to be used for reading, to light something, or for anything else. They are only for the mitzvah.

5. The Chanukah candles must stay lit for at least half an hour after dark.

Did You Know??
We use olive oil because the miracle of the Menorah in the *Beis HaMikdash* happened with olive oil.

A Closer Look
The *shamash* should be higher or lower than the other flames. This shows that the *shamash* is not one of the Chanukah lights. The *shamash* may be used for other purposes.

6. On Chanukah it is customary to eat potato latkes or fried jelly donuts.

A Closer Look
These foods are fried in oil, which reminds us of the miracle of oil that happened on Chanukah.

7. It is customary to eat dairy foods on Chanukah, since Yehudis fed cheese to the Greek general to make him thirsty. Then she gave him wine to drink. When he fell asleep from the wine, she killed him.

8. It is customary for children to play dreidel on Chanukah.

Did You Know??
Outside Eretz Yisrael, the letters ש, ה, ג, נ, are written on the four sides of the dreidel. This stands for the words, נֵס גָּדוֹל הָיָה שָׁם — a great miracle happened there. In Eretz Yisrael, the letter פ appears on the dreidel instead of the letter ש. The פ stands for the word פה which means "here." Thus the four letters stand for נֵס גָּדוֹל הָיָה פה — A great miracle happened **here**, because the Chanukah miracle happened in *Eretz Yisrael*.
This dreidel reminds us how children at the time of the Chanukah story would gather together secretly to learn Torah. If they heard soldiers coming, they would start playing with the dreidels to make it seem as though they were only playing games. The dreidel is also a way of teaching little children about the miracle of Chanukah.

Did You Know??
The prayer *Al HaNissim* tells about the miracle of Chanukah — how Hashem helped the weak and the few righteous people defeat the many and strong evil people.

9. On Chanukah we add the prayer *"Al HaNissim"* when we say the *Shemoneh Esrei* and in *Birkas HaMazon*.

Purim
HASHEM SAVES THE JEWISH PEOPLE

King Achashverosh sat on his throne in Shushan, the capital city of Persia. "I am the most powerful man in the whole world," he thought. "I rule 127 countries from India to Ethiopia. I will make a huge party to show everyone how rich and strong I am."

It was a magnificent party. For six months people ate and drank as much as they could. Even the gold and silver vessels which had been stolen from the *Beis HaMikdash* many years earlier, were shown off at this party.

Afterwards, the king made a second party, just for the people of Shushan. Achashverosh became very drunk. "Bring Vashti the queen to me now," he barked. "I want everyone to see how beautiful my wife is."

But Vashti would not come. "Who does he think he is?" thought Vashti. "Who is he to order me around like this? I am the Queen of Persia!"

Did You Know??
King Solomon built the first *Beis HaMikdash* in Jerusalem. For 410 year the Jewish people served Hashem there. Then, King Nevuchadnezzar came from Babylonia and destroyed the Temple and exiled the Jews to Babylonia. Fifty-one years later, the armies of Persia came and defeated the Babylonians. Many of the Jews from Babylonia were then brought to Persia.

A Closer Look
Vashti, the granddaughter of Nevuchadnezzar, was a very wicked woman. She forced Jewish girls to do hard work for her, especially on Shabbos. Also, she helped convince the king not to let the Jews rebuild the *Beis HaMikdash* in Jerusalem.

When Achashverosh was told that Vashti would not come, he became furious. He met with his wise men. They said the queen should be killed for ignoring his command. Achashverosh ordered his men to kill her.

After he killed Vashti, King Achashverosh was very sad and lonely. "Your Highness, we will search the entire kingdom for a beautiful new queen for you," advised his servants. This idea made the king very happy.

Women came from all over the kingdom, and the king's officers even forced women to come. But the king could not find the one who he felt should be his queen.

The king's officers brought a Jewish lady named Esther. When Achashverosh saw her, he immediately decided that she would be his queen.

Esther was the cousin of Mordechai, a great rabbi and the leader of the Jews who lived in Shushan. He was a member of the Great Sanhedrin, the Jewish High Court, and all the people respected him. "Do not tell the king that you are Jewish," Mordechai warned Esther. She listened to everything he told her.

A Closer Look
While at the palace, Esther made sure to eat only kosher food. She also kept the holy Shabbos.

Did You Know??
Esther's parents were not alive, so Mordechai raised her in his own home. Esther also had another name, Hadassah.

One day, while sitting at the king's gate, Mordechai overheard two servants, Bigsan and Seresh, plotting to kill the king. Immediately, he reported this to Esther, who quickly told the king about it, in Mordechai's name. The king had the story checked out, and it was proven to be true. "Let these two servants be killed!" ordered the king.

The story of how Mordechai saved the king was then written in the king's diary.

A wicked man named Haman became King Achashverosh's second-in-command. Haman was the one who told Achashverosh to kill Vashti for not coming to the party.

Did You Know??
The two servants spoke together in a language called Tarsi. They thought no one would understand them. But because Mordechai was a member of the Sanhedrin, he understood all seventy languages and knew what they were saying.

"Everyone must bow down to me when I walk down the street," Haman demanded. But Mordechai would not bow down. This made Haman very angry. "I will kill Mordechai and all the Jewish people," he decided.

Haman made a lottery to decide what date would be the best to kill all the Jews. He picked the 13th day of Adar, the twelfth month of the year.

After he picked the date , Haman rushed to Achashverosh to tell him about his idea. "A certain group of people live in your kingdom who are different than all the others," Haman explained. "They follow their own laws and do not listen to the laws of the king. That is bad for your kingdom — I think you should destroy them. If you do, I will personally add ten thousand pieces of silver to your royal treasury."

The king quickly agreed. "Take my royal ring, and do whatever you please," he told Haman. With the king's ring, Haman could make any law he wanted. "As for the silver, you can keep that for yourself."

Did You Know??
The ten thousand pieces of silver that Haman offered Achashverosh was equal to 750 tons of silver — an enormous amount of money!
Haman thought Adar would be a good month to kill the Jews, because that is the month when Moshe *Rabbeinu* died. Haman did not know that Moshe *Rabbeinu* was also born in Adar! Moshe *Rabbeinu* was born and died on the same date — the 7th day of Adar.

Did You Know??
Haman had an idol sewn onto his clothing. That is why Mordechai would not bow down to him.
Haman was a descendent of Amalek, the grandson of Eisav. Eisav and Amalek, and the nations who carried their names, always hated the Jewish People. After the Exodus from Egypt, Amalek was the first nation that attacked the Jewish People in the desert.

A Closer Look
King Achashverosh hated the Jews. He was more than happy to have Haman destroy them.

Haman called together the king's scribes. "Write a letter today, in the name of the king, to the rulers of every land, saying that all the Jews should be killed on the 13th day of the month of Adar." He stamped the letters with the king's official seal. The letter was sent out a few days before Pesach. The 13th of Adar would be eleven months later.

When the Jews of Shushan saw this letter posted on the walls they became confused.

A Closer Look
Why does the Megillah say that the Jewish people were confused? They should have been scared! This was because many of the Jews had stopped acting like Jews. They acted like Persians, and they thought of themselves as Persians, not Jews. They could not believe that the Persians would want to kill them.

When Mordechai heard about the decree, he tore his clothing and put sackcloth and ashes on himself. "You must repent," he told the Jewish People. "Only Hashem can stop Haman and his evil plan." The Jews fasted and cried, begging Hashem to save them.

Mordechai sent Esther a message about the evil decree. He said, "You must go before the king and beg him to tear up the evil decree."

Did You Know??
Mordechai wanted Esther to understand that even though she was Queen, this would not be enough to save her from Haman's evil decree.

"No one is allowed to go to the king unless he calls them — not even I!" Esther explained. "If I go on my own, I may be killed!" But Mordechai insisted. "Hashem has many ways to save His People," he explained. "Either you go or Hashem will help some other way. But you will miss your chance! Maybe this is why Hashem made you the Queen."

A Closer Look
Tens of thousands of Jews gathered together in the center of Shushan. Mordechai read from a Torah which was wrapped in shrouds. He read the section telling the Jewish people how Hashem would punish them if they sinned.

"Then tell the people to fast and pray for three days," Esther requested. "No one should eat or drink. Then I will go before the king and do as you ask."

On the third day, Esther dressed in her royal clothing and approached the King. "I know that the king can have me killed for doing this, but I must do what I can to help my people," she thought.

Achashverosh was very surprised to see her. He lifted his scepter and told her to approach. "What does my queen request?" he asked. "You can have anything you desire, even up to half of my kingdom."

"If it pleases the king," Esther replied, "I would like the king and Haman to come today to a special party that I have prepared."

"Tell Haman to hurry, and together we will go to the Queen's party, just as she requested," Achashverosh said.

Later, at the party, the king again asked, "Esther, tell me what it is that you want. You can have anything you desire, even up to half of my kingdom."

Esther looked at the King. "It is my wish," she said, "that you and Haman come to a second party tomorrow. Then I will tell the king everything he wishes to know."

A Closer Look
Esther wanted Haman to be at the party so that she would be able to set a trap for him.

Did You Know??
The king was constantly trying to find out who Esther really was and who her people were. Esther meant that at the party she would finally tell him.

When he left the party, Haman was in a very good mood, until he saw Mordechai, who refused to bow to him. Then he ran home and called for his wife and his friends.

He bragged to them about how rich and powerful he was. Even Queen Esther was inviting him to her private parties! But he was still so angry that Mordechai would not bow down to him. What could he do?

"Why not build a high gallows? In the morning you can ask the king for permission to hang Mordechai on it," they said. "Then you will be happy!" Haman could not wait till the morning. He decided to make the gallows right away and rush to the king in middle of the night to ask for permission to hang Mordechai.

While this was happening in Haman's house, the king could not sleep. He asked that his personal diary be brought and read to him.

The king listened to the stories being read to him. He heard the story of how Mordechai had saved his life from Bigsan and Seresh.

"What was done to honor Mordechai for saving my life?" asked the king.

"Nothing," replied the servant.

Just then Haman entered the king's courtyard. The king called for him to come in.

"Haman," the king asked, "what shall we do for a man the king wishes to honor?"

A big smile appeared on Haman's face. "No doubt it is *me* whom the king wishes to honor, since I am his favorite servant," he thought.

He said, "The person the king wishes to honor should be dressed in royal garments, and led on the royal horse through the street by an important servant who will call out, 'This is what is done to the man whom the king wishes to honor.'"

A Closer Look
This was a very busy night. Esther was busy preparing for her party, Mordechai was busy learning and praying, Haman was busy building the gallows, and the king was busy having his diary read to him.

A Closer Look
Step by step, Haman is being brought closer to his final downfall.

Did You Know??
When Haman's daughter heard someone calling, "This is what is done to the man whom the king wishes to honor," she was sure it was Mordechai honoring her father. She threw a pot of rotten garbage onto the man leading the horse. When she realized that it was her father, she jumped from the roof and died.

"Then hurry up. Get the royal garments and the horse that you spoke about, and do everything you said — all of it — to Mordechai, the Jew!" ordered the king. "Make sure you don't leave anything out!"

Haman was shocked. He didn't want to honor his enemy, but he had to do what the king ordered. He dressed Mordechai in the royal garments and led him through the streets on the royal horse, announcing, "This is what is done to the man whom the King wishes to honor."

Haman returned home very sad. Zeresh, his wife, said to him, "Once you have begun to lose to Mordechai, who is a Jew, you will not be able to succeed against him. You will continue to fall!"

As soon as she finished speaking, the king's guards came to rush Haman to Esther's party.

Esther's second party began. "Tell me, my queen," begged Achashverosh, "what is it you want? I will give you even up to half of my kingdom."

"Now I will tell you," replied Esther. "It is not for myself that I ask, but for my people. There is an evil person who wishes to destroy my nation. Please, O King, save my people!"

"Who is the person who dares to do such a thing?" the king roared.

"It is none other than this wicked man, this evil Haman," Esther replied.

The king's face twisted in anger. Haman begged for his life to be saved. Charvonah, a servant in the palace, pointed to the gallows that Haman had just built, and said, "Look, Haman even plotted to kill Mordechai, the person who saved the king's life."

"Take Haman," shouted the king, "and hang him from the gallows."

After Haman was hanged, Esther brought Mordechai to the king and explained that he was her relative. "You can have all of Haman's property," Achashverosh said to Esther and Mordechai. And the king gave the royal ring to Mordechai, making him the most powerful person in the land.

But Haman's decree to kill the Jews was still the law. So Esther went back to Achashverosh and asked him to save her people. The king said that she and Mordechai could write a new law.

Mordechai and Esther sent a new letter throughout the land, telling everyone that on the 13th day of Adar — the day on which Haman had planned for the Jews to be killed — the Jews could defend themselves. They could now destroy anyone who attacked them.

On that day, the Jews in each city got together and defeated all the enemies who wanted to kill them. In Shushan, the Jews killed 500 men, including the ten sons of Haman.

Did You Know??
Haman was hanged on a gallows that was 50 *amos* high (about 100 feet). It was so high that everyone in Shushan was able to see what had become of the enemy of the Jews.

Did You Know??
The 500 people killed in Shushan were all descendents of Amalek.
Haman was hanged in the month of Nissan, during Pesach. The Jews got to defend themselves 11 months later, on the 13th of Adar.

In the rest of the Persian Empire, another 75,000 people were killed.

All this happened on the thirteenth day of Adar. The Jews rested on the next day, the fourteenth, and celebrated it as a happy day, giving presents and charity.

In Shushan, the capital, Esther asked for permission for the Jews to kill their enemies on the next day, too. She also wanted Haman's ten sons to be hanged on the gallows that Haman had made for Mordechai. In that city, the fighting continued into the fourteenth day of Adar, and they celebrated on the fifteenth.

The Rabbis established that the fourteenth of Adar should be the holiday of Purim. In Shushan and in cities that had walls around them at the time the Jews first entered *Eretz Yisrael* in the time of Yehoshua, the Rabbis said that the fifteenth of Adar should be Purim. Jerusalem is such a city.

The Jews were once again saved by Hashem.

A Closer Look
Although Hashem's Name is never mentioned in the Megillah, we constantly see His Hand guiding all the events. Nothing happened by chance. Everything was planned by Hashem.

A Closer Look
The same people who wanted to destroy the Jews were now destroyed themselves.

LAWS OF PURIM

1. Purim is celebrated on the fourteenth day of Adar. Our Sages teach us that the month of Adar is a month of joy for the Jewish people.

2. The thirteenth day of Adar is a day of fasting. It is called *Ta'anis Esther*.

Did You Know??

The Jewish People usually fasted on the day when they fought their enemies. Also, Queen Esther asked the Jews to fast and pray for three days and nights before she went to speak to King Achashverosh. Even though that fast was not in Adar (it was actually in the month of Nissan), we fast just before Purim, the holiday that celebrates the miracle that came through Esther's going to the king.

A Closer Look

Instead of being killed, the Jews were allowed to kill their enemies on the thirteenth day of Adar. They celebrated their victory on the fourteenth day, which is now the holiday called Purim. In Shushan, the capital city, the Jews were allowed to kill their enemies on the fourteenth day of Adar. Therefore, they celebrated on the fifteenth day of Adar as well, which is called Shushan Purim.

Our Sages made a rule that all cities that were — like Shushan — surrounded by a wall, should celebrate Purim on the fifteenth of Adar. But at that time, *Eretz Yisrael* was in ruins, and our Sages didn't want only cities outside *Eretz Yisrael* to have this special status. So they decided that any city that had a wall in the time of Yehoshua (which is when the Jews conquered Eretz Yisrael over 900 years earlier) would celebrate Purim on the fifteenth day of Adar, just like Shushan. Jerusalem is the only city that we know for sure had a wall then, and Purim there is celebrated on Shushan Purim — the fifteenth of Adar.

3. On Purim, Megillas Esther is read from a parchment scroll. It is read at night and again in the morning.

4. Before Purim begins, it is customary to give what is called *machatzis hashekel* — a coin that is worth half of the type of money used in that place — to charity.

Did You Know??
The Megillah tells the story of Purim. When people hear the name Haman, they make noise or stamp their feet to "wipe out" his name. Haman came from Amalek, the nation that is the eternal enemy of the Jewish people.
The person reading the Megillah recites the names of Haman's ten sons in one breath. This is because they were all hanged at the same time.

Did You Know??
People give half of whichever kind of money is used in their country. Depending on where they live, they will give either a half-dollar, a half-pound, a half-shekel, or a half-ruble.
This half-dollar reminds us of the half-shekel that was given in the time of the *Beis HaMikdash*, during the month of Adar, for buying public sacrifices. The custom is to give three half-dollars

Did You Know??
Al HaNissim tells us about the miracle of Purim — how Haman tried to destroy the Jewish People, but Hashem saved us and destroyed Haman and his sons instead.

5. On Purim we add the prayer *"Al HaNissim"* when we say the *Shemoneh Esrei* and *Birkas HaMazon*.

6. On Purim we must send two ready-to-eat foods to at least one friend. This is called *Mishloach Manos*. We are also required to give charity to at least two poor people. This is called *Matanos L'Evyonim*.

Did You Know??
Both men and women are required to give *Mishloach Manos* and *Matanos L'Evyonim*. Our Sages teach us that it is more important to give charity to poor people on Purim than to have a very fancy *Mishloach Manos* or Purim meal.

7. We celebrate Purim by being happy, eating, and drinking wine.

Did You Know??
During the day of Purim we must eat *Seudas Purim* — a special Purim meal.

8. It is also customary, especially for children, to dress up in costumes and masquerade as different characters on Purim. We then go to people's houses to sing and dance and make merry.

Did You Know??
Some give this reason for why people dress up: The miracle of Purim is different from many other miracles, in that the Hand of Hashem was hidden throughout the entire story. To remember this, we "hide" behind our costumes.

Pesach
The Exodus From Egypt

"our children will be strangers in a strange land," Hashem told Avraham Avinu. "They will be slaves and suffer. All of this will happen over a period of four hundred years. In the end, they will go free and be wealthy. And I will punish the nation that made them slaves."

About two hundred and twenty years later, there was no food in many lands, including the land of Canaan, where Avraham's grandson Yaakov and his children lived. Yaakov and his sons then went down to Egypt so they would not starve. They lived in the Goshen section of Egypt.

A Closer Look

The Jews' move to Egypt began 22 years earlier, when Yaakov's sons sold their brother Yosef as a slave, and he was brought down to Egypt.

In Egypt, Yosef was falsely accused of a crime and thrown into prison. While there, he correctly explained the dreams of two servants of Pharaoh. Later, when Pharaoh had a dream that no one could explain, he was told about Yosef, who was brought to interpret Pharaoh's dream.

Yosef said that Egypt would have seven years of extra food, then seven years of hunger. He told Pharaoh to store food during the first seven years, so there would be plenty to eat and sell later. Pharaoh said that if Yosef was smart enough to understand the dreams, he should be in charge of the country. When Yaakov and his sons later came down to Egypt, Yosef arranged for them to live in the land of Goshen, and he made sure they had everything they needed.

Years later, after all of Yaakov's sons died, a new king arose to rule Egypt. He did not care about all the good things that Yosef had done for Egypt; how Yosef saved the entire land from starving, and made Pharaoh rich by selling food for a lot of money.

"There are too many Jews!" Pharaoh complained to his advisors. Hashem had blessed the Jewish People, and the women were giving birth to six babies at one time! "Let us outsmart the Jews," Pharaoh said, "and make them our slaves."

And so they did. The Jewish People became slaves in the land of Egypt, doing hard, backbreaking work.

But the Egyptians were still worried. They saw more and more Jews living among them. One day, Pharaoh's astrologers made a shocking prediction: "We see that a Jewish baby will soon be born who will free the Jewish People and lead them out of Egypt!"

"We cannot allow that," shouted the King. "All Jewish baby boys will be thrown into the Nile River and drowned."

Did You Know??
Pharaoh commanded the Jewish midwives to kill all the Jewish boys as soon as they were born. But Yocheved and her daughter, Miriam, the two Jewish midwives, did not listen. "There is nothing we can do," they told Pharaoh. "The Jewish women are very smart and run off to the field and give birth there before we even arrive." This way they were able to save many Jewish babies. Since Yocheved and Miriam did not help him, Pharaoh ordered his soldiers to throw all Jewish baby boys into the River.

One night, Yocheved, the midwife, gave birth to a baby boy. "What will we do with our baby?" Yocheved asked her husband, Amram. "The Egyptian soldiers will surely find him and throw him into the Nile River!"

For three months Yocheved hid the baby in her home. Then it became too dangerous. She placed him into a basket and put the basket on the River. "Let us pray that Hashem will save him," Yocheved thought.

Miriam kept watch over her baby brother as he floated on the river in his little basket.

Bisya, the daughter of Pharaoh, was on her way to bathe in the River. "What is that?" she asked her servants when she saw the basket. Bisya stretched out her arm and grabbed the basket. Inside, she saw a beautiful little baby who was crying. She could tell he was Jewish. Bisya pitied the tiny baby.

Bisya told her servants to feed the baby, but he refused to eat. Then Miriam came to Bisya and said, "Maybe I should call a Jewish woman to feed him?." Bisya agreed, and Miraim brought Yocheved, who then raised the baby in her own home.

When the baby got a bit older, he was brought back to Pharaoh's palace. "I will call him Moshe," Bisya stated, "because it means 'drawn' and he was drawn from the water.'"

Did You Know??
Moshe was born on the 7th day of Adar in the year 2368 from when the world was created.

Moshe was raised as a prince in the royal palace. The people there loved to play with him. Once, when he was still very young, he was sitting on Pharaoh's lap. Suddenly, Moshe grabbed Pharaoh's crown and put it on his own head.

All the ministers and servants stared in shock. "This is a sign that he will rebel against Pharaoh some day!" they said.

They decided to give the child a test to see if he knew what he was doing. They placed gold and red hot coals on a tray. Then they placed the tray in front of Moshe. "Let us see if he can tell what is truly valuable, or if he just wants anything that is shiny," they said. "If he takes the gold, we will know that he took Pharaoh's crown on purpose."

Moshe began to grab the gold, but an angel came and pushed his hand onto the burning coal. Moshe, still holding the coal, then stuck his hand into his mouth and he burnt his tongue. From that time onward, he did not speak clearly.

Moshe grew into a young man. He knew he was Jewish and wanted to see how his fellow Jews were being treated. One day he went walking among the slaves. He saw an Egyptian man beating a Jewish slave. Moshe ran over and killed the Egyptian. The next day Moshe tried to break up a fight between two Jewish men. The two men were Dassan and Aviram. They were bad people. "What are you going to do to us?" asked Dassan. "Will you kill us also, the way you killed the Egyptian?"

Pharaoh also heard about the story, and he wanted to have Moshe killed. Moshe realized that he could no longer stay in Egypt.

Moshe ran away from Egypt and arrived in Midian. He saw a group of shepherds chasing away some women who were trying to draw water from a well. Moshe saved the women from the shepherds and gave water to the sheep. These women were the daughters of Yisro, a Midianite priest. Moshe later married one of Yisro's daughters, Tzipporah.

In Egypt, the situation of the Jews grew worse every day. They prayed to Hashem to save them from their misery and take them out of Egypt. Hashem heard their prayers. He was now ready to choose His messenger to save the Jewish People.

One day, while Moshe followed a lost lamb through the desert, he saw a thorn bush that seemed to be on fire. There was fire, but the bush was not being burnt! Moshe approached the bush. Suddenly he heard a Voice from inside the bush.

A Closer Look
Hashem appeared to Moshe in a thorn bush, the lowliest of trees. He later appeared on Mount Sinai, one of the smallest mountains, to give us the Torah. This teaches us to be humble.

Did You Know??
The burning bush that Moshe saw was at Mount Sinai, where Hashem would one day give His Torah to the Jewish People.

"Moshe, Moshe," the Voice called.

"Here I am," Moshe replied.

"Do not come any closer," the Voice continued. "Take off your shoes. The ground that you are standing on is holy! I am the G-d of your fathers, the G-d of Avraham, the G-d of Yitzchak, and the G-d of Yaakov."

Moshe was terrified. He was afraid to look at the burning bush.

"I have seen the suffering of My people in Egypt," Hashem said. "I will bring them out of Egypt to a land that is flowing with milk and honey. I will send you as My messenger to Pharaoh, and you will take My people out of Egypt."

"But who am I to go to Pharaoh?" Moshe replied.

"I will be with you," said Hashem. "Just go and tell the people that I have sent you to save them. But you should know that Pharaoh will not send out My people easily. In the end I will do great wonders against the Egyptians."

Did You Know??
The staff in Moshe's hand first belonged to Adam *HaRishon*, and it was passed down through the generations until it reached Avraham, Yitzchak, and Yaakov. Later on it reached Moshe. This is the same staff that *Mashiach* will one day hold when the Jewish People are again redeemed.

Since Moshe insisted that he was not worthy, Hashem sent Moshe's older brother, Aharon, along with him to speak to the Jewish People and to Pharaoh.

Moshe and Aharon arrived in Pharaoh's palace. "Hashem, the G-d of Israel, has sent us to you to command you to let His people out of Egypt so that they can worship Him in the desert!"

Pharaoh laughed at them. "Who is your G-d that I should listen to

Did You Know??
Moshe was 80 years old when he came to Pharaoh's palace. Aharon was 83 years old.

Him?" Pharaoh then decreed that the work the Jews were doing should be made even harder. He said they were lazy and just wanted an excuse not to work. "They want to leave Egypt? I will teach them!" he declared.

Until then, the Egyptians gave the Jews straw that they needed to make bricks. But Pharaoh wanted them to work harder. "Do not give them straw. Let them make the same amount of bricks, but let them find their own straw."

This made some Jews angry at Moshe and Aharon. "You came to save us?" they complained. "You are just making us work even harder!"

Then Hashem told Moshe that He would bring plagues to force Pharaoh to let the Jews go.

Hashem told Moshe, "Tell Aharon to stretch out his staff over the Nile River and hit it. All the water in Egypt will turn into blood! Even the water in the Egyptian's drinking cups!"

Aharon struck the River with his staff and all the water in Egypt turned to blood. All the fish in the water died and began to smell bad. This plague lasted for seven days.

Did You Know??
Water that belonged to Jews did not become blood. If an Egyptian took water from a Jew, it became blood; but if he bought the water from a Jew, it remained water. Hashem told Aharon, not Moshe, to strike the water. The water that had saved Moshe when he was a baby, floating on the river in a basket, so it was not right for Moshe to strike water. This teaches us to always be grateful to anyone who does us a favor.

In all, Hashem brought ten plagues on the Egyptians: 1) blood 2) frogs 3) lice 4) wild animals 5) the domestic animals died 6) boils 7) hail 8) locusts 9) darkness 10) the death of the firstborn.

 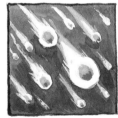   

Finally, after the tenth plague, the killing of every firstborn Egyptian, Pharaoh called to Moshe, "Leave Egypt at once, you and all the Jews!"

Did You Know??
Exactly at midnight of the 15th of Nissan, Hashem killed all the Egyptian firstborn.

A Closer Look
The Jews were commanded to bring a *Korban Pesach*. They had to slaughter a sheep, and put some of the blood on their doorframes. Then Hashem would skip their houses during the tenth plague when all Egyptian firstborn would be killed. This *korban* (sacrifice) was then eaten by the Jews at their Passover meal on the night before they left Egypt, on the 15th of Nissan.
The holiday is called Pesach, which means Passover, because Hashem "passed over" the Jewish houses when He killed the Egyptian firstborn.
It took a lot of courage for the Jews to slaughter the sheep, because the Egyptians worshiped sheep, and they would try to harm anyone who killed their god.

Moshe had told the Jews, "The time of our freedom has arrived. With a strong hand and an outstretched arm, Hashem will take us out of Egypt, and bring us to the Land of Israel."

The Egyptians chased the Jews out of Egypt. They did not even have enough time to let their dough rise. Instead of becoming bread, it was matzah.

A Closer Look
Hashem had told Avraham that the Jews would be strangers for 400 years. But Hashem took them out of Egypt after 210 years, because in His kindness, He began counting the 400 years from the birth of Yitzchak. Also, the Jews had to work so hard in Egypt, that the 210 years were like 400 years.

Did You Know??
This flat bread that did not have time to rise is called matzah. On Pesach we eat matzah to remember how quickly we left Egypt.
Six hundred thousand Jewish men between the ages of twenty and sixty left Egypt on Pesach. All together, including the older and younger men, the women, and the children, there were about three million people.

After the Jews left, Pharaoh changed his mind. "What have we done?" he shouted. "How could we have let the Jews leave our land? Who will do all our work for us?" Pharaoh himself hitched up his own chariot and led the way. His whole army — including all the chariots in Egypt — followed to chase after the Jews.

The Children of Israel were encamped by the Sea of Reeds. When they saw Pharaoh's army coming, they were afraid. "We have nowhere to go," they cried out to Moshe. "The Egyptians are behind us and the Sea is in front of us. At our side is the desert. Why did you take us out of Egypt to just die here in the desert?"

"Do not fear!"commanded Moses. "Hashem will fight this war for you. Now you will see His true strength and glory."

Then, Moshe stretched out his staff over the sea. A strong east wind blew the whole night. Moshe told the people to walk right into the sea. Nachshon, the leader of the tribe of Yehudah, jumped into the water until it was up to his nose — and then the sea split.

The Jews crossed the Sea of Reeds on dry land.

Did You Know??
As soon as the Jews left Egypt, a miraculous pillar of cloud had appeared in front of them, to lead them. As they were camped at the Sea, with the Egyptians coming up behind them, this cloud moved behind the Jews, and stood between them and the Egyptians. The clouds made it dark for the Egyptians and swallowed up all the Egyptian arrows and stones.

A Closer Look
The Sea divided into twelve different sections, with each tribe crossing in its own lane.

Did You Know??
The Jews crossed the Sea of Reeds on the 21st day of Nissan, which is now the seventh day of Pesach.
After they passed through the Sea, the Jews sang a song of praise to Hashem. Then Moshe's sister, Miriam led the women in song and dance to praise Hashem.

The Egyptian army now followed the Jews down onto the dry bed of the sea. When the Jews had all crossed the dried Sea, Hashem commanded Moshe, "Spread out your hand again over the Sea." As soon as he did, the waters caved in on the entire Egyptian army, drowning them all.

Moshe led the Jewish People in song, praising Hashem for splitting the sea and saving them from the Egyptians.

Pesach is a spiritual holiday when we celebrate our freedom from Egypt and slavery. But it is also the holiday when we celebrate the ripening of our winter crops, and when the fruit trees begin to blossom. Our Rabbis teach us that our success in this world is totally dependent on Hashem's blessing. There is no clearer place to see this than with a farmer's crops. He needs Hashem to give rain and the right kind of weather. In the same way, all our success in this world comes only from Hashem's blessings.

LAWS OF PESACH

1. On Pesach, the Jewish people celebrate being freed from slavery in Egypt. The Torah tells us that Pesach begins on the fifteenth of Nissan, the day that Hashem took us out of Egypt.

2. Before Pesach, we give *maos chittim,* a special charity, to help those who cannot afford food for Pesach.

Did You Know??
The words *maos chittim* mean "wheat money." This special charity has this name because it gives poor people enough money to buy matzos (which are usually made from wheat), and other food for Pesach.

A Closer Look
When we are satisfied and happy, we must also make sure that people who have less than we do are also happy. We must care not only about ourselves; we must care about others, too.

3. Before Pesach we clean our homes to make sure there is no *chametz* left there. *Chametz* is anything that has in it food made from grain that has become leavened. Bread and cookies are such foods. Many things we do not think of as being foods are also *chametz*.

A Closer Look
We are not allowed to own any *chametz* during Pesach, even if we do not eat it. Pesach cleaning is not just spring cleaning, it is cleaning to make sure we properly keep this mitzvah.

4. The night before Pesach, after the house has been cleaned, we check to make sure that we didn't miss any *chametz*. This is called *Bedikas Chametz* (Searching for the *Chametz*). This is a thorough search that includes every place where *chametz* may be, including drawers, pockets, corners, and places where *chametz* may have fallen. We even check our cars!

To best check these places, the Sages tell us to use a regular candle that gives off light but does not have a large flame. This is so that we will look carefully into all the little spaces without being afraid of causing a fire. Today, some people use a flashight. We must always be very careful not to cause a fire.

After the search we declare that any *chametz* we do not know about is not ours anymore.

Did You Know??
It is customary to use a feather and wooden spoon in the search. The feather is meant to be used to sweep the *chametz*, and all its crumbs, into the spoon. We collect all this *chametz*, the feather, and the spoon and put them aside to be burned in the morning.

A Closer Look
There is a custom to spread ten small pieces of bread around the house before the search begins. This guarantees that the father will find some chametz during the search. In many houses the children are the ones to put it out.

5. We are not allowed to eat, or even own, any *chametz* on Pesach.

A Closer Look
After suffering the Ten Plagues, the Egyptians chased the Jewish people out of Egypt. The dough that the people were baking had no time to rise. So the Jewish people brought this flat bread (matzah) with them into the desert.

6. There is a custom for all firstborn boys and men to fast on the day before Pesach. If a boy is too young to fast, his father should fast for him.

A Closer Look
This is to remind us that on the night before the Jews left Egypt, Hashem killed all the Egyptian firstborn, while the Jewish firstborn were saved.

Did You Know??
In most communities, the firstborn attend a *siyum*, the completion of a section of the Talmud. Since a *siyum* is a mitzvah, and this is a special type of fast day, even the firstborn are allowed to eat from the *siyum* meal. Once they eat at a mitzvah celebration, the first-born are allowed to eat for the rest of the day as well.

7. The Torah says that we are not allowed to own *chametz* on Pesach, even if we will not eat it. That means that all *chametz* must be eaten, given away, thrown away, destroyed, or burned before Pesach. A person may also sell his *chametz* to a non-Jew.

Did You Know??
This is a complicated sale, so people appoint their rabbi to sell their *chametz* for them. All the *chametz* that is still in the house is put away and becomes the property of the non-Jew who buys it. The rabbi then buys it back after Pesach.

8. On the morning before Pesach, any *chametz* that will not be sold, including the ten pieces of *chametz* found during the search the night before, is burned. Then, we announce that any *chametz* we still have in our possession no longer belongs to us, and is as if it no longer exists.

9. We do not eat matzah on the day before Pesach. Many people have a custom of not eating matzah for thirty days before Pesach.

Did You Know??
This way, the matzah eaten at the Seder will taste special, and we will really enjoy it.

Did You Know??
The word *"seder"* means order. Our Sages arranged the order of the *Haggadah* so we would know exactly how to perform all the speical mitzvos we have that night (for example: telling the story of Pesach, drinking the four cups of wine, eating matzah and *maror,* etc.).

10. Jews who live outside Israel have a Seder on the first two nights of Pesach. Jews who live in Israel have a Seder only on the first night.

A Closer Look
While the Jews were still in Egypt, Hashem commanded that on the afternoon of the 14th of Nissan, groups of people should get together and slaughter a lamb. They were to roast it and eat it that evening. This was called a *Korban Pesach.* Later, once the Jews entered *Eretz Yisrael,* they brought the *Korban Pesach* at the *Mishkan,* and in later years, at the *Beis HaMikdash.* The *korban* was slaughtered on the afternoon before Pesach and eaten at the Seder.

Did You Know??
In Israel, Pesach is seven days, not eight. Only the first and seventh days of Pesach are Yom Tov, and the middle five days are Chol HaMoed.

11. It is customary for married men to wear a white *kittel* at the Seder.

12. We put a plate with three matzos on the table at the Seder. Some communities use only two matzos.

Did You Know??
Many reasons are given for using three matzos.

A main reason is that we are supposed to say the Haggadah with a broken matzah in front of us, so we break one matzah at *yachatz*. But we still need two whole matzos for when we wash and make the *berachah Hamotzi*, later in the Seder.

Some of the other reasons given are that the three matzos represent the three groups of Jews: Kohen, Levi, and Yisrael; that they are to remember that Avraham Avinu asked Sarah to prepare three measures of flour for the angels who came to visit them on Pesach; and they remind us that it was in the merit of our three *Avos* (Avraham, Yitzchak, and Yaakov) that Hashem took us out of Egypt.

13. The matzos at the Seder that are used for the *mitzvah* must be "*shemurah*" matzah. Many people eat only matzah that is "*shemurah*" through all of Pesach.

A Closer Look
Shemurah means guarded. *Shemurah* matzah is made with flour that is guarded from when the grain is cut in the fields. If the grain never gets wet, we can be sure that it did not become *chametz*. The laws of eating *chametz* are very strict; some people eat only *shemurah matzah* all of Pesach, to be extra careful.

14. We arrange a special plate, called the *Ka'arah,* to be used at the Seder.

A Closer Look

The Seder plate contains the foods that are talked about during the Seder. Some of these foods will be eaten during the Seder.

a) and b) *Maror* and *Chazeres* — Bitter Herbs. These remind us of the bitter life the Jewish people had in Egypt. It is eaten twice after the matzah (once alone, and once in a sandwich with matzah).

c) *Karpas* — This is a vegetable that is eaten at the beginning of the Seder. It is dipped in salt water to remind us of the tears the Jewish people cried in Egypt.

d) *Charoses* — This is a mixture of grated apples, dates, chopped nuts, cinnamon, and red wine. It reminds us of the clay that the Jews used to build cities for the Egyptians. We dip the *maror* into the *charoses* before we eat the *maror,* to make sure that we are not hurt by the *maror's* sharpness.

e) *Zero'a* — Shankbone: in the time of the *Beis HaMikdash,* two offerings were brought on the afternoon before Pesach: the *Korban Pesach* and the *Korban Chagigah.* Their meat was roasted and eaten at the Seder feast. The *Zero'a* — a bone with some meat on it — is roasted over the fire, like the Pesach offering. We do not eat it at the Seder, because we cannot bring a Pesach offering when we don't have the *Beis HaMikdash.* The roasted *Zero'a* reminds us of the *Korban Pesach.*

Also, the word *zero'a* means arm. This reminds us that Hashem took us out of Egypt with an outstretched and mighty arm.

f) *Beitzah* — Hard-boiled or Roasted Egg: this reminds us of the *Chagigah* offering that was brought in the *Beis HaMikdash* in honor of Yom Tov. Most people have the custom of eating the egg at the start of *Shulchan Oreich,* — the actual meal of the Seder.

15. Men must lean to their left side when drinking the four cups of wine and while eating the matzah, *korech,* and *afikoman.* Many say the Haggadah and eat their meal while leaning.

Did You Know??
Only royalty (and not slaves) have the luxury of leaning while they are eating. During the Seder, the Jewish people act like royalty, to symbolize their freedom.

A Closer Look
We do not lean while eating the *maror,* because that reminds us of the bitterness of working for the Egyptians, when we were slaves.

16. At four specific points throughout the Seder, we drink a cup of wine, for a total of four cups.

Did You Know??
The four cups remind us of the four words of salvation Hashem used when telling Moshe about the Jews leaving Egypt. They are: 1) וְהוֹצֵאתִי — *I will take you out,* 2) וְהִצַּלְתִּי — *I will save you,* 3) וְגָאַלְתִּי — *I will redeem you,* 4) וְלָקַחְתִּי — *I will take you as My chosen people.*

17. At the Seder a young child asks the Four Questions.

18. Toward the beginning of the Seder, at *Yachatz*, a piece of matzah called the "*afikoman*" is put aside to be eaten at the end of the Seder meal.

19. After the *afikoman* is eaten, we are not allowed to eat any more food.

A Closer Look
There is a custom that the children "steal" the afikoman and hide it. When it is time to eat it, the father, "buys it back" by offering the children a prize. There are different versions of this custom as well.
This is done to make sure the children stay up until the end of the Seder meal.

A Closer Look
There are two reasons why we eat the *afikoman* at the end of the meal:
a) It reminds us of the Pesach offering, which was the last thing eaten at the Pesach meal.
b) This way, the taste of the matzah stays in our mouths as long as possible.

Lag Ba'Omer
Rabbi Akiva and His Students

About 2,000 years ago, there was an ignorant but honest shepherd named Akiva. Each day he faithfully took care of his flock of sheep. Once, when he was forty years old, he noticed how dripping water had made a hole in a rock. "If the water can make a hole and penetrate into that rock," he thought, "then surely the Torah can enter into my heart." He immediately went to the yeshivah of Rabbi Eliezer and began learning Torah. He eventually became the leading rabbi of his generation.

A Closer Look
Rabbi Akiva was held in such honor that the other Sages ruled that whenever there is a dispute between Rabbi Akiva and one of the other Sages, the law follows Rabbi Akiva's opinion.

Did You Know??
Rabbi Akiva, who came from a family of converts, married a woman named Rachel. She was from a very rich and respected family. Her father, Kalba Savua, did not want Rachel to marry Akiva. "He is a poor ignorant shepherd, you cannot marry someone like him!" he shouted in anger. But Akiva had agreed that if Rachel married him he would go study in yeshivah. After they married, her father made them leave his home. She and Akiva were very poor, but Akiva went off to yeshivah. He came back after 12 years. When he reached the door of his home, he heard her say that she would like him to learn for another 12 years. He immediately returned to his yeshivah for another 12 years. Finally, after 24 years, he returned home with thousands of students. "Whatever I have and whatever you have learned from me is because of her," he explained to his students. "She is the one who sent me to study Torah."

Rabbi Akiva had 24,000 students, and they all died during the *Sefirah* period, between Pesach and Shavuos. Our Rabbis teach that they died because they did not respect each other enough. They only died on 33 days during this period, so the 33rd day of the Omer is a happy day. Ashkenazic communities make weddings, take haircuts and listen to music on Lag Ba'Omer. Sephardic communities wait until the next day.

With so many students no longer alive, all of Torah could have been lost. But Rabbi Akiva began to teach a new group of students, and the study of the holy Torah continued.

A Closer Look
The students of Rabbi Akiva were not at all cruel and nasty to one other. In fact, by our standards, they were very respectful of each other. But *tzaddikim* are judged on a much different and higher level than we are. Considering their high level, they should have given one another even more honor.

The Romans outlawed the study of Torah. "Anyone who studies Torah, anyone who teaches Torah, and anyone who follows the laws of the Torah will be put to death," they proclaimed. But Rabbi Akiva continued to teach Torah anyway. Eventually he was caught by the Romans and tortured him to death. His dying words were, *"Shema Yisrael Hashem Elokeinu Hashem Echad* — Hear O Israel, Hashem is our G-d, Hashem is One."

A Closer Look
Rabbi Shimon bar Yochai was one of the later students of Rabbi Akiva. The Romans wanted to arrest him, so R' Shimon and his son R' Elazar hid in a cave for 13 years. They studied Torah the entire time. A miracle happened and a carob tree and a stream of water were created right next to them so they could eat and drink. Finally, Eliyahu *HaNavi* came to the opening of the cave and announced, "The Roman Emperor has died. It is now safe for you to come out."

Did You Know??
On the day of R' Shimon bar Yochai's death, he revealed many secrets of the Torah to his students. These were written down in a book called the *Zohar*. R' Shimon said that the Jewish People should celebrate that day because of all the Torah he taught. That day was Lag B'Omer, the eighteenth day of Iyar.

COUNTING THE OMER AND LAG BA'OMER

1. We begin counting the *Omer* on the second night of Pesach. We continue to count every night until the night before Shavuos (forty-nine days later).

Did You Know??
These seven weeks, when we count the *Omer*, are the same seven weeks in which the Jews in the desert prepared themselves to receive the Torah from Hashem at Har Sinai.

When the *Beis HaMikdash* stood, the Jewish People started this counting period by bringing the *Omer* (the first barley offering), and on Shavuos, after completing the counting, they brought the *Sh'tei HaLechem* (Two Loaves), baked from the first wheat harvest.

These seven weeks used to be a very happy time. It reminded the Jewish People of the Exodus and the giving of the Torah. Later these seven weeks became a sad time for the Jewish people. The fact that we cannot bring the *Omer* anymore reminds us that we no longer have the *Beis HaMikdash*. Also, during thirty-three days of the *Omer* period, the thousands of students of Rabbi Akiva died. Over a thousand years later, about 800 years ago, during the Crusades, many Jews were murdered in Europe duirng the time of *Sefirah*.

A Closer Look
The Omer was an offering from the first barley harvest of the year. It was brought in the *Beis HaMikdash* on the second day of Pesach. The Torah commands us to count forty-nine days (seven weeks) from then, and the holiday of Shavuos is celebrated on the fiftieth day. This time period is called *Sefiras HaOmer* — the Counting of the *Omer*.

2. A blessing is said each night before the *Omer* is counted. We recite the blessing:

בָּרוּךְ אַתָּה ה׳ אֱלֹהֵינוּ מֶלֶךְ הָעוֹלָם, אֲשֶׁר קִדְּשָׁנוּ בְּמִצְוֹתָיו וְצִוָּנוּ עַל סְפִירַת הָעוֹמֶר.

Blessed are You, Hashem, our God, King of the universe, Who has made us holy with His mitzvos, and commanded us about counting the Omer.

3. We count the Omer while standing. We count it every evening. If we forgot to count at night, we should still count on the next day, but without saying a *berachah*. Then, on the following evening, we can again continue counting with a *berachah*. If we forgot to count for a whole day, we continue counting the rest of the days, but without a *berachah*.

A Closer Look
We count how many days, then how many weeks and days, have passed since we began counting. For example, on the eighth night we say "tonight is the eighth night, which is one week and one day in the Omer." We then ask that Hashem return the *Beis HaMikdash* to us very soon.

4. For at least 33 days during the seven weeks of the *Omer*, we mourn the death of Rabbi Akiva's students. We do not take haircuts, make weddings, or listen to music.

Did You Know??
There are different customs about which 33 days are days of mourning. Here are some of the main customs: Some communities start with the first day and mourn until Lag B'Omer; some mourn until the 34th day of the *Omer*; some mourn from Rosh Chodesh Iyar to the *Sheloshes Yemei Hagbalah* (The three days before Shavuos), except for Lag B'Omer; and some mourn the entire period, except for special days like *Yom Tov,* Lag B'Omer, Rosh Chodesh, and the *Sheloshes Yemei Hagbalah* — this leaves exactly 33 days of mourning.

Shavuos

Hashem Gives the Torah to the Jewish People

Between Pesach and Shavuos

After the sea split and the Egyptian army drowned, the Jews were now ready to receive the Torah and be led by Hashem into *Eretz Yisrael.*

For three days they wandered in the Wilderness till they came to a place called Marah. The people were thirsty but could not drink the water because it was bitter. "What shall we drink?" the people complained to Moshe.

Did You Know??
The word Marah means bitter.

Hashem showed Moshe a piece of wood. Moshe threw it into the water, and the water became sweet and good to drink.

As the Jewish People continued wandering in the desert they became hungry. "If only we had died in Egypt," they complained. "There, at least we had food. Here, we will die of starvation!"

"Behold," Hashem called out. "Food will rain down from heaven. Each day the people will take what they need for that day, and on Friday they will take an extra portion for Shabbos."

A Closer Look??
This food from heaven was called *mann.* The miracle of *mann* teaches us that we should never lose faith in Hashem. No matter how much trouble we are in, Hashem can save us, just as He saved the Jews in the desert.

A Closer Look

Every day an enormous amount of *mann* fell on the ground. No matter how much a person gathered, everyone ended up with the same amount. All of the uncollected *mann* was gone by the afternoon. If someone tried to save some for the next day, it spoiled. The next morning more *mann* would fall. This taught the Jewish People to trust in Hashem every single day.

Each Friday, a double portion of mann would fall — one for Friday and one for Shabbos. Since one is not allowed to carry outside on Shabbos, the *mann* for Shabbos fell on Friday.

The more righteous a person was, the closer to his tent his *mann* would fall. The most righteous people found it right outside their door, the wicked people had to walk very far.

Did You Know??

Aharon filled a jar with the *mann* and placed it in front of the Holy Ark. It was brought into *Eretz Yisrael* and was placed in the *Beis HaMikdash*. This way future generations would be able to actually see the miracle that Hashem had done.

The *mann* fell for forty years, until the Jews arrived at the border of *Eretz Yisrael*. The last day's *mann* did not spoil — the Jews kept on eating from it until they were able to use the new harvest!

Since a double portion of *mann* fell on Friday, in honor of Shabbos, we make *Hamotzi* on two challos on Shabbos. This is called *Lechem Mishneh,* which means double bread.

The Jews continued their journey in the desert. They arrived at Rephidim and again there was no water. "Give us water so that we will not die here in the desert," they begged. Hashem commanded Moshe to strike a rock with his staff and fresh water came pouring from the rock.

Did You Know??

While the Jews were camped in Rephidim, the nation of Amalek attacked them. The Jews won the battle, but this was the first time since the Jews had left Egypt that a nation dared to attack them. Even though the Jews won the battle against Amalek, now — because Amalek attacked — other nations felt they could also fight the Jews. Hashem told us to remember what Amalek did in the desert. We are commanded to wage war against Amalek for all time, until they are totally destroyed.

Over nine hundred years later, Haman, a descendent of Amalek, would again try to destroy the Jewish People.

Receiving the Torah on Mount Sinai

After more than five weeks of wandering in the desert, the Jewish People arrived in the Sinai Desert and set up camp there. It was the first day of Sivan. Hashem was preparing to give the Torah to the Jewish People.

A Closer Look
Hashem had approached all the nations of the world and asked each one, "Do you want to accept My Torah?" The descendents of Eisav asked, "What is written in this Torah?" "You shall not kill," Hashem said. "We cannot accept the Torah," they answered. "We live by the sword." Then Hashem asked the children of Ishmael to accept the Torah. "What is written in it?" they asked. "You shall not steal," they were told. "We cannot accept that. We live by stealing." Every nation was asked, and every nation refused the Torah. When it was offered to the Jews, they immediately said, "Everything that Hashem has said, we will do and we will hear." The Jewish People did not even ask what was written in the Torah. They trusted Hashem, and they accepted His Word right away.

Hashem commanded Moshe to tell the Jews, "You have seen what I have done for you in Egypt. If you listen to Me and observe My commandments, you shall always be My beloved people."

All the people answered, "All that Hashem has spoken, we shall do."

"Let the people make themselves holy today and tomorrow," Hashem said. "On the third day I will show My Glory to the people, on Mount Sinai. Let no one, not even an animal, touch the mountain, or even come too close to the mountain."

A Closer Look
There were over 600,000 adult men at Mount Sinai. All together, there were over three million people there. The soul of every Jew ever to be born was also there (your soul, too!).
Each one of these three million people saw what happened when Hashem gave the Torah on Mount Sinai. They did not need anyone to tell them that Hashem gave the Torah, because they saw it themselves. Each of them told their children, who told their children, up until today, more than three thousand years later. No other religion has ever claimed that millions of people heard the words of Hashem directly; only the Jewish People.

Did You Know??
On Shavuos we celebrate that Hashem gave the Jewish People His holy Torah.

It was Shabbos morning, the seventh day of Sivan, in the year 2448. There was thunder and lightning. A heavy cloud rested on Mount Sinai. There was a very loud sound of the shofar and all the people trembled in fear. The mountain shook and smoke came billowing out. Hashem's Presence was on the mountain. The sound of the shofar grew louder and louder.

Moshe went up the mountain, and Hashem began stating the Ten Commandments.

Did You Know??
Hashem stated the first two of the Ten Commandments, but it was too holy for the people. They begged Moshe to speak to them instead of Hashem, because they were afraid they would die.

When Hashem began speaking, no other sound was heard throughout the whole world. No bird chirped, no river flowed, no animal made a noise. There was complete silence.

A Closer Look
Not only did the people see the lightning, but they actually saw the thunder and the sound of the shofar too! This was a great miracle, because they saw things that we only hear. We can't see thunder.

"Climb up Mount Sinai where I will teach you My laws," Hashem commanded Moshe. "Meanwhile, Aharon, his older sons Nadav and Avihu, and the seventy elders should stand on the side of the mountain."

Moshe remained on the mountain for forty days and forty nights. Hashem taught him the whole Torah. He also taught him the Oral Torah, which explains everything in the Torah.

Did You Know??
There is a special mitzvah to remember the giving of the Torah at Mount Sinai.

On Yom Kippur, Moshe came down from Mount Sinai with the second tablets of the Ten Commandments (See Yom Kippur page 17).

A Closer Look
The Torah is the most important thing to the Jewish People. It is compared to water because just as we cannot live without water, we cannot live without the Torah.

The Torah is also the blueprint for the world. Hashem looked into His Torah and made the world so that we could keep the Torah's mitzvos.

But the people made a terrible mistake. Forty days after they heard the Ten Commandments, they expected Moshe to come down from the mountain. They thought Moshe was late in coming down from Mount Sinai. They became nervous. "Aharon" they cried, "we do not know what happened to Moshe. Make a god to lead us."

"Give me all your gold," Aharon told them. Aharon wrapped up all the gold and threw it into a fire. It melted and a golden calf arose out of the flames.

Hashem then said to Moshe, "Go down now and see how wicked your people have become. They have made a golden calf and are bowing to it. This is such a terrible sin that they deserve to be destroyed!"

Moshe begged Hashem to forgive them. "If you kill the Jewish People now, the nations of the world will say You took them out of Egypt to destroy them in the desert. Have pity on the Jewish People for the sake of Avraham, Yitzchak, and Yaakov." Hashem wanted Moshe to pray for the people, and He listened to Moshe.

Moshe climbed down the mountain with two stone tablets in his hand. On both sides of these stones were the Ten Commandments written by Hashem. Moshe saw the people dancing around the Golden Calf and worshiping it. He became very angry. He threw down the Ten Commandments and shattered them. "Whoever is for Hashem, come to me," he shouted. All the Leviim gathered around him. The three thousand people who had worshiped the Golden Calf that day were put to death.

A Closer Look
Aharon was really trying to delay the people until Moshe returned. He thought the people, especially the women and children, would not give their jewelry. But the other people took the gold by force.

Moshe climbed Mount Sinai a second time to pray to Hashem to forgive the Jewish People. He prayed there for forty days and forty nights, until Hashem said that He would forgive them. When Moshe came down, Hashem told him to prepare stone tablets, and He would write the Ten Commandments on them. Moshe went back up the mountain, where, for the next forty days and nights, Hashem taught him the Torah again.

Shavuos is a spiritual holiday — a celebration of the day the Jews received the Torah from Hashem. The Torah also describes it as *Chag HaHatzir* — celebration of the cutting down of the fully grown crops in the field.

Did You Know??
Shavuos is the only holiday for which the Torah does not give the calendar date. It is always on the fiftieth day from the start of the *Omer* count, which begins on Pesach. This teaches us that the entire purpose of our being freed from Egypt on Pesach was to receive the Torah from Hashem seven weeks later, on Shavuos.

LAWS OF SHAVUOS

1. We started counting the forty-nine days of the *Omer* on the second night of Pesach. *Shavuos* is the day after the *Omer* count ends.

A Closer Look
The Torah commands us to count the days from Pesach until Shavuos. In the desert, the Jews couldn't wait to receive the Torah. They were so excited that they counted each day, starting from Pesach, waiting for Hashem to give them the Torah. On each day, they worked to improve themselves so they would deserve to receive the Torah.

Did You Know??
On Shavuos Hashem gave the Jewish People the Torah on Mount Sinai, seven weeks after He took them out of Egypt.

The word Shavuos means "weeks." Shavuos is called the Festival of Weeks because it comes after counting seven weeks from Pesach.

Shavuos is also called *Chag HaBikkurim* — the Festival of the First Fruits — because on Shavuos the *Shtei Halechem*, an offering of two loaves of bread made from the new wheat crop, would be brought in the *Beis HaMikdash*. Also, the *Bikkurim*, the first ripe fruits of the *Shiv'as HaMinim* (Seven Species of Eretz Yisrael) had to be brought to the *Beis HaMikdash* as a gift to the Kohanim. A Jew could begin bringing his *Bikkurim* each year at Shavuos. When the *Bikkurim* was given to the Kohen, the farmer would thank Hashem for taking us out of Egypt and giving us *Eretz Yisrael*.

Shavuos is also called *Chag HaKatzir* — the Festival of the Harvest — because that is the time of year when the crops are harvested.

Shavuos is also called *Atzeres*. It is like Shemini Atzeres, the day that finishes the happy festival of Succos. Shavuos finishes the festival of Pesach, because the only reason we were taken from Egypt was to receive the Torah on Shavuos.

In all our prayers, we call Shavuos *Z'man Mattan Toraseinu* — the Time of the Giving of our Torah — because that is when the Torah was given on Mount Sinai.

2. Shavuos is celebrated on the sixth day of Sivan. Outside of *Eretz Yisrael* it is celebrated for two days, the sixth and seventh of Sivan.

3. On Shavuos night it is customary to stay up all night and learn Torah.

Did You Know??
The Jewish people slept the night before the Torah was given, and Hashem had to wait for them to arise in order to give the Torah. To make up for this mistake we stay up and learn all night.

4. We read the Book of Ruth on Shavuos.

Did You Know??
There are a number of reasons for reading the Book of Ruth on Shavuos. Some are: The story of Ruth took place during the harvest season, and Shavuos is the time of the harvest. Also, Ruth, a convert to Judaism, accepted Hashem's Torah. This is what all the Jews did when they accepted the Torah. Another reason is that, as the Book of Ruth tells us, Ruth was a great-grandmother of David *HaMelech*. Shavuos is the day David *HaMelech* was born, and he died on Shavuos 70 years later.

5. On Shavuos, we read the poem *Akdamus* in shul.

6. It is customary to eat dairy products on Shavuos.

A Closer Look
When the Torah was given, the Jewish People found out how to prepare meat so that it is kosher. This takes time. Until they were able to prepare kosher meat, they ate only dairy food.

7. In many communities, it is customary to decorate the shul with grass, flowers, branches, and leaves on Shavuos.

Did You Know??
Akdamus, a poem by R' Meir ben Yitzchak, was written in the 11th century, as an introduction to the Ten Commandments. It praises Hashem, His Torah, and the Jewish people. It tells us that even if all the heavens were paper, all the forests were pens, all the oceans were ink, and all the people in the world were writers, we would still not be able to tell how great Hashem is.
Akdamus is not written in Hebrew, but in Aramaic.

A Closer Look
The grass reminds us of how Mount Sinai (where the Torah was given) was covered with grass. Also, the fruits of the trees are judged by Hashem on Shavuos.

Tishah B'Av

The Jewish People are Punished in the Desert

After Moshe came with the second set of Tablets of the Ten Commandments, He told the Jews how Hashem commanded them to build the *Mishkan*. This would be Hashem's "dwelling place" on earth. A person would be able to feel Hashem's Presence there, because that was where the Tablets were kept and that is where the Kohanim served Hashem by bringing *korbanos,* offerings to Hashem, for the Jewish People. Every time they moved to a new place in the desert, they took apart the *Mishkan*. The Levi'im carried the parts to the next place, where it was together again.

When the Jews entered *Eretz Yisrael*, they established the *Mishkan* at Gilgal. It took fourteen years for the Jews to conquer *Eretz Yisrael* and divide the Land among the tribes. After that they established the *Mishkan* at Shilo.

After 369 years, the *Mishkan* in Shilo was destroyed in a war with the Pelishtim. For the next 57 years, there was no permanent *Mishkan*. The Kohanim brought the *korbanos* in Nov and Giv'on.

In his fourth year as King of Israel, Shlomo began building the *Beis HaMikdash*. This would replace the *Mishkan* as the new "dwelling place" of Hashem on earth. He finished the *Beis HaMikdash* 480 years after the Jews left Egypt.

Did You Know??
The *Beis HaMikdash* could not be built by King David, (Shlomo's father), because he had been involved in too many wars. Hashem wanted the *Beis HaMikdash* to be a House of Peace.
No iron tools were used to build the *Mishkan* or the *Beis HaMikdash*, because iron is used to make weapons that kill people. An unusual worm called the *shamir* was used to cut through the stone.

Did You Know??
The Torah never says exactly where the *Beis HaMikdash* should be built. It always says, "the place that Hashem will choose."

The First Beis HaMikdash

With great celebration, dancing and singing, after seven years of work, King Shlomo dedicated the First *Beis HaMikdash*. But after he died, the Jewish People split into two separate kingdoms, Yehudah and Yisrael. Many of the people began to worship idols, especially in the kingdom of Yisrael. Instead of working to make the people better, many of the kings sinned and caused others to sin, as well.

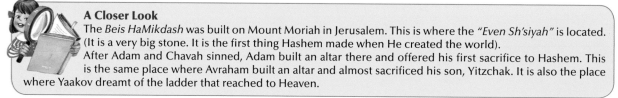

A Closer Look
The *Beis HaMikdash* was built on Mount Moriah in Jerusalem. This is where the *"Even Sh'siyah"* is located. (It is a very big stone. It is the first thing Hashem made when He created the world).
After Adam and Chavah sinned, Adam built an altar there and offered his first sacrifice to Hashem. This is the same place where Avraham built an altar and almost sacrificed his son, Yitzchak. It is also the place where Yaakov dreamt of the ladder that reached to Heaven.

Over the next several hundred years, there were many kings in each of the two kingdoms. One of the most righteous of all the kings was Yoshiyahu.

Yoshiyahu, one of the kings of Yehudah, became king at the very young age of eight. He was a very good person who decided to make much needed repairs in the *Beis HaMikdash*. In the 18th year of his rule, the *Kohen Gadol* found a *Sefer Torah* and brought it to the king. It was read to him and he led the people in repenting from their evil ways. He removed all the idols from the Temple and throughout the kingdom.

Sadly, after 31 years, Yoshiyahu was killed in battle against the Egyptians. Once again, the kings after him began to do evil and worship idols.

Yirmiyahu the prophet warned everyone, "If you do not repent, you and Jerusalem will be destroyed. Return to the ways of Hashem and you will be saved." But the people did not listen to him. The king even threw him into jail! During this time, Nevuchadnezzar became king of Bavel.

At the age of 21, Tzidkiyahu became the new king of Israel. He was a good man. He ruled for the final eleven years before Nevuchadnezzar destroyed the Temple and Jerusalem.

A Closer Look
Yirmiyahu tried to convince King Tzidkiyahu to accept the rule of Babylonia over Israel. "This will be the punishment for all their sins, such as idolatry," he explained. But Tzidkiyahu did not listen. He decided to rebel against Nevuchadnezzar, King of Babylonia.

Did You Know??
The First *Beis HaMikdash* stood for 410 years. It was destroyed on the ninth day of Av, in the year 3338.
Our Rabbis teach us that the First *Beis HaMikdash* was destroyed because of three terrible sins that the people committed: idol worship, immorality, and murder.

A Closer Look
In two long chapters of the Torah, Hashem warns the Jewish People of terrible punishments that will happen to them if they do not follow His ways. These chapters are called the *tochachah*. These punishments are meant to awaken the Jewish people and encourage them to repent.

Did You Know??
When the Jewish People were in the desert after leaving Egypt, Moshe sent twelve men to spy on the land of Canaan. They returned and reported, "The people there are powerful giants. We are like grasshoppers compared to them. We will never be able to defeat them." The Jewish People cried that whole night. That night was Tishah B'Av, the Ninth of Av. Hashem punished the Jewish People by keeping them in the desert for forty years. From then on, Tishah B'Av has always been a sad day for the Jewish People.

Jerusalem was under siege. There was no food or water. The people were dying of thirst and starvation. On the ninth day of Tammuz, the Babylonians broke through the walls of the city of Jerusalem.

Did You Know??
The Assyrian army, led by Sancheirev, also tried to destroy Jerusalem over 100 years earlier. Nevuchaznezzar knew how Hashem had destroyed the Assyrian army with a plague in just one night. He was afraid the same thing could happen to him. He therefore sent his general, Nevuzaradan, to attack the city for him.

After the Babylonians broke through the outer walls of the city, King Tzidkiyahu realized there was no hope. He tried escaping through an underground water tunnel that was eighteen miles long, and opened near the city of Yericho. But Hashem made sure that Babylonian soldiers would be chasing a deer near the exit of the tunnel so they would see Tzidkiyahu coming out. He was captured and brought to Nevuchadnezzar. Nevuchadnezzar slaughtered all ten sons of Tzikdiyahu, then blinded him, and led him away to Babylonia in chains. He died there.

Nevuchadnezzar's army, led by Nevuzaradan, then entered Jerusalem. On Tishah B'Av, the ninth day of the month of Av, they destroyed the *Beis Hamikdash.*

A Closer Look
It only seemed as if Nevuchadnezzar and the Babylonians were the ones who controlled the destruction of the Temple. Really they were only messengers of Hashem. It was the sins of the Jewish People that caused the Temple to be destroyed.

Did You Know??
After destroying Jerusalem and the *Beis HaMikdash*, and after slaughtering so many Jews, Nevuzaradan eventually repented and converted to Judaism!
The exile after the destruction lasted for seventy years. The miracle of Purim happened during those years.

The Second Beis HaMikdash

When the Jews were building the Second *Beis HaMikdash,* they were ruled by foreign kings. The Persian King Darius, who, some say, was the son of Queen Esther, gave the Jews permission to rebuild the Temple in Jerusalem. Even after they built the Temple, they were still under Persian rule for many, many years. Then the Jews continued to use the Temple under the rule of the Syrian-Greeks. But the Syrians used the *Beis HaMikdash* for idol worship. When the five sons of Matisyahu defeated the Syrians (see Chanukah, page 35), the Jews finally became independent of foreign rule.

Unfortunately, the descendants of Matisyahu's sons were not good and righteous. They did not follow the ways of Hashem.

> **Did You Know??**
> Hyrkanus and Aristobulus were brothers who were descendants of the Chashmonaim. Each of them wanted to be king. One brother and his men ruled inside Jerusalem, so his brother's army surrounded the city. Every day, the people inside the city would lower a basket of coins over the wall, and those outside would send up an animal that would be brought for the daily sacrifice in the *Beis HaMikdash.* One day those outside the city were told that they would not be able to defeat those inside the city as long as they were offering sacrifices to Hashem. So the next day, instead of sending up a kosher animal, they sent up a pig. When the pig's hoofs touched the city's wall, the entire country shook. This was the beginning of the end of Jewish rule.

Rome soon began to rule the land of Israel. They made Herod the king. Herod was a cruel murderer, whom the people feared. He even killed almost all of the great Sages. But he did do one good thing. He rebuilt the Second *Beis HaMikdash* and made it very beautiful.

> **Did You Know??**
> The Jews had built the Second *Beis HaMikdash* hundreds of years before Herod, but it had become run down over the years. Herod took thousands of workers and repaired and rebuilt the *Beis HaMikdash.* But then he did a terrible thing. He placed a gold eagle, the symbol of the Rome, right over the entrance gate of the Temple.

A Closer Look

The Gemara teaches us that Jerusalem was destroyed through the following incident: A man had a friend named Kamtza and an enemy named Bar Kamtza. The man sent someone to invite Kamtza to a party. By mistake, though, his servant invited Bar Kamtza, his enemy. "Why are you here? Get out!" the host shouted at Bar Kamtza. "But I am here already," replied Bar Kamtza. "Please, do not embarrass me by throwing me out in front of everyone!" Bar Kamtza even offered to pay for the whole party, but the host insisted that Bar Kamtza leave.

Bar Kamtza became furious at the man and furious at the rabbis who were at the party but did not help him. "I will get my revenge," he thought. Bar Kamtza went to the Emperor of Rome and told him that the Jews were rebelling against him! The emperor believed him. This drew the Jewish nation closer to their destruction.

There remained one last hope for the Jewish People: Agrippa, Herod's grandson. When he became king, he tried to listen to the Sages and the laws of the Torah. His enemies were angry that he allowed the Jewish community to grow in strength, and they poisoned him.

The Romans oppressed the people more and more. But even worse, the Jews were fighting among themselves. Jews hated other Jews. It was because of this hatred that Hashem decreed that the Second *Beis HaMikdash* would be destroyed.

The Roman army surrounded Jerusalem. Its commander was General Vespasian. He wanted to capture the city and destroy the *Beis HaMikdash.*

Rabbi Yochanan ben Zakkai was the head of the Sanhedrin in Jerusalem. "Sneak me out of Jerusalem," he told his students. "I want to speak with Vespasian."

When he finally reached the general, Rabbi Yochanan ben Zakkai said, "Peace be with you, O Emperor."

"Why do you call me Emperor?" Vespasian asked.

"Because soon you will be Emperor," he replied.

While they were still talking, a messenger came to tell Vespasian that he had just been chosen to be Emperor of Rome. Vespasian was overjoyed. As a reward he granted three wishes to Rabbi Yochanan. Rabbi Yochanan asked that Yavneh and the Sages there be spared. Second, he asked that the family of Rabbi Shimon ben Gamliel not be killed. Rabbi Shimon was the leader of the Jewish People and a descendant of King David. And finally, he requested that the great and pious Rabbi Tzadok of Jerusalem be treated by a doctor. Rabbi Tzadok was sick because he had been fasting and praying for so many years, begging Hashem to save Jerusalem and the *Beis HaMikdash.*

A Closer Look
No Jews were allowed to leave Jerusalem. Rabbi Yochanan ben Zakkai told his students to tell everyone he was sick. A few days later, they announced that he had died. His students placed him into a coffin to bring him out of Jerusalem to bury him. That is how he was able to get out of the city to meet Vespasian.

Vespasian returned to Rome. He was replaced by his son Titus, who led an army of 80,000 soldiers to defeat Jerusalem. It was a bitter and bloody war, with many people dying. Titus decided to starve the Jews. No food was allowed into the city. On the seventeenth day of Tammuz, the Roman army finally broke through the walls of Jerusalem. For three weeks the Jewish People fought courageously. Then, on the ninth day of Av, the Romans broke into the Temple Mount and completely destroyed the Second *Beis HaMikdash*. Fires were set everywhere. All the vessels of the Holy Temple were stolen and brought back to Rome, along with many prisoners who became slaves.

Did You Know??
It was on Tishah B'Av, 420 years after it was built, that the Second *Beis HaMikdash* was destroyed.
Over one million Jews died during the period of the Destruction of the Second *Beis HaMikdash*.

Did You Know??
Hashem promised that some of the Western Wall of the *Beis HaMikdash* will never be destroyed. The *Shechinah* (Hashem's Holy Presence) has never left that holy place.

A Closer Look
Five terrible things happened on Tishah B'Av: 1) In the time of Moshe *Rabbeinu*, it was decreed that the Jews in the desert would not enter *Eretz Yisrael*; 2) The First *Beis HaMikdash* was destroyed; 3) The Second *Beis HaMikdash* was destroyed; 4) The city of Betar was conquered and its people killed; 5) The wicked Turnus Rufus plowed up the area where the *Beis HaMikdash* had stood.
The Second *Beis HaMikdash* was destroyed because people hated each other for no reason.
Today, a shul or yeshivah is considered a *mikdash me'at*, sort of a miniature Temple. There, we can pray to Hashem, study Torah, and feel closer to Him.

LAWS OF TISHA B'AV AND PUBLIC FAST DAYS

1. Our Sages said we should fast on certain days of the year — these are days when we are not allowed to eat or drink.

Did You Know??
A person is not required to fast until reaching the age of Bar or Bas Mitzvah. But even a person who may eat on a fast day, such as a child or a sick person, should try not to eat special foods like ice cream and cake.

A Closer Look
These days are times of sadness in Jewish history. On these days we think about how to become closer to Hashem and how to better follow His laws.

2. The public fast days are:

   a. The Fast of Gedaliah on the third day of Tishrei.

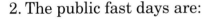

Did You Know??
After the first *Beis HaMikdash* was destroyed by Nevuchadnezzar, Gedaliah ben Achikam, a righteous Jew, was made governor for the Jewish people who still lived in *Eretz Yisrael*. But a Jewish traitor killed Gedaliah. The remaining Jewish people were killed or forced to leave the country.

   b. The Tenth of Teves.

Did You Know??
On this day, the evil Nevuchadnezzar surrounded the city of Jerusalem. It was the beginning of his attack on Jerusalem and the *Beis HaMikdash,* which ended with the destruction of the *Beis HaMikdash* and the exile of the Jewish people from *Eretz Yisrael*.

   c. The Seventeenth of Tammuz.

Did You Know??
Five very sad things happened on this day: 1) When Moshe came down from Mount Sinai and saw the Jews dancing around the Golden Calf, he smashed the Tablets containing the *Aseres HaDibros* (Ten Commandments); 2) In the time of the First *Beis HaMikdash,* the Jewish People were forced to stop offering the daily sacrifice; 3) During the destruction of the Second *Beis HaMikdash*, the Romans broke through the walls of Jerusalem; 4) The evil Roman General Apostamus burned a Torah Scroll; 5) An idol was put in the *Beis HaMikdash*.

d. Tishah B'Av (The Ninth of Av).

3. Of these 4 fast days, all except Tishah B'Av begin in the morning. Tishah B'Av begins at sundown of the 8th of Av. On Tishah B'Av, we are also not allowed to wash ourselves or wear leather shoes. Until midday on Tishah B'av, we sit on the floor or on low chairs, like mourners.

> **Did You Know??**
> Five very sad things happened on this day: 1) the spies that Moshe sent to observe the Land of Israel returned and told the people that they would not be able to conquer the land. The Jewish people believed them and cried; 2 and 3) the First and Second *Beis HaMikdash* were destroyed; 4) the city of Beitar was destroyed by the Romans and its people were killed; 5) the Romans plowed over the ruins of the Second *Beis HaMikdash*.

4. On Tishah B'Av evening, we sit on the floor or on low chairs and listen to Megillas Eichah being read. It sadly tells us of the terrible things that happened to our people. Then we read *Kinnos* (sad poems).

5. At *Shacharis* of Tishah B'Av, we do not put on *tallis* or *tefillin*. At the end of *Shacharis,* we recite *Kinnos*. These sad peoms discuss how terrible the destruction of the *Beis HaMikdash* was, and about many of the troubles Jews have suffered during this long Exile. *Tallis* and *tefillin* are put on for *Minchah*.

6. We do not make weddings or other happy celebrations between the Seventeenth of Tammuz and Tishah B'Av.

> **A Closer Look**
> This period of time, which is called The Three Weeks, is a very sad time for the Jewish people. We do not take haircuts, shave, listen to music, or make celebrations. From Rosh Chodesh Av to Tishah B'Av we do not eat meat (except on Shabbos) or bathe for pleasure. We wash up for Shabbos as we usually do. Most Sefardic communities practice all these limitations only during the week of Tishah B'av.

7. In addition to the above fasts, which are all related to the destruction of the *Beis HaMikdash*, we also fast on Taanis Esther, the day before Purim (or on Thursday before Purim, if Purim is on Sunday).

> **Did You Know??**
> Taanis Esther recalls how the Jews fasted and prayed on the thirteenth of Adar when they battled their enemies, and how Queen Esther and all the Jews fasted and prayed for three days, so Hashem would save the Jewish People.

8. Yom Kippur is the most important fast day of the year. It is when Hashem seals our fate for the coming year in the Book of Life. It is not a sad day at all. It is a day to repent and have our sins forgiven.

> **Did You Know??**
> Yom Kippur is the only fast day that is commanded in the Torah (For more on Yom Kippur, go to page 17).

This volume is part of
THE ARTSCROLL SERIES®
an ongoing project of
translations, commentaries and expositions
on Scripture, Mishnah, Talmud, Halachah,
liturgy, history, the classic Rabbinic writings,
biographies and thought.

For a brochure of current publications
visit your local Hebrew bookseller
or contact the publisher:

Me'sorah Publications, ltd

4401 Second Avenue
Brooklyn, New York 11232
(718) 921-9000
www.artscroll.com